Saving Mr. Johnson
Red Hats in Love Mystery #1

Alyne Bailey

Publisher's Note:

This is a work of fiction. All names, characters, places, and events are the work of the author's imagination.

Any resemblance to real persons, places, or events is coincidental.

Solstice Publishing - http://www.solsticeempire.com/

Chapter One

When I was a young woman just after World War Two, I thought it was such fun to share an apartment with my friend Myrtle Anderson Bailey. We had recently graduated from high school, had jobs, and together could afford our rent. I'm sure our parents were both proud and terrified for us on our own. It was a tiny space on the second floor above the furniture store. The bedroom was just large enough for two twin beds. The closet was equally tiny, but neither of us had more than two or three dresses. My father wished that I had lived at home until I was ready to marry. My mother was the one who helped us find that apartment and convinced the landlord that we were 'good girls.' There really was no reason for them to have worried. Our time in that apartment gives me many good memories.

Now, sixty-five years later, Myrtle and I, plus many of our friends, have apartments in the St. James. It is a beautiful–five-story brick apartment house built in the 1920's, and has been totally updated by the son of one of our residents. It is located between Meeker and James Street in downtown Kent, Washington, a suburb south of Seattle. Being downtown means we are within walking distance of shops and restaurants. There are days when I miss the little house I shared with my late husband, George. We had a beautiful garden. The young couple who bought the house still send pictures of the flowers that I had planted. At eighty-six, I'm not sure my knees could handle working in the garden any longer. I've turned my attention to baking cookies. My friends seem to enjoy the results.

Red Hat Day is our monthly event to dress up in our 'Sunday best' dresses, don our fancy red hats and slowly walk over to one of the many restaurants in the area for lunch. Our Red Hat Society ™Chapter is made up of the residents of our building as well as a few select friends. Having an entire building occupied by 70 to 90-year-old women may sound dull, but that couldn't be farther from the truth. It doesn't hurt that the manager is Mr. Johnson. Why would that be special? Simply because he is 70, alive, single and likes women. Over the last five years, he has dated many of the residents.

I am still dressing when there is loud knocking on my door. "Mable Schmidel, did you hear?" Asks Betty Stiles in her overly loud excited teacher voice as soon as I open my door. She is dressed in her standard uniform of a dark pleated skirt and white blouse with a Peter Pan collar. I always wonder about just how many of them she must have. Her short cap of white hair is topped by a red beret with hand sewn sequins. She may dress like a 'little old lady,' but she acts more like a steam roller as she charges into my foyer. She stops to put both hands on her hips. "Elsie Hansen's husband has died. Did you even know that she was married?" Of course, I had just gotten her text. Nothing that goes on in the St. James is beyond the 'little old lady network' as that dear girl Claire Murphy Thompson has called it. There is something to be said for that network, although some days privacy seems like a good idea. Betty is followed closely by Myrtle and Hattie Hoy. Florence Thompson must have heard the commotion, because she steps out of her apartment next door. I still miss having Claire live next door, but I'm also happy that her mother-in-law, Florence has taken that apartment.

The other women are collected in the hallway between the fifth-floor elevator and my front door. I stand back to waive them on into my apartment. Florence and I are fortunate to have the largest units in the building. We each have two bedrooms where the other units are only one bedroom with four units per floor except ours. Because they are here often, each woman goes to her favorite place in my living room. Today, Hattie's brightly flowered orange and teal dress clashes with both her purple and teal mohawk mullet and my mauve pink chair. Florence neatly arranges her navy-blue dress as she sits. Myrtle, in contrast, paces in front of my large wall of windows. Because I am so much taller than Betty, I take a chair so I can look at her face when I ask, "You sent me a text without any details. Where did you get this information? Did Elsie tell you?" If I had been standing, I wouldn't have seen Betty's frown.

Betty's frown turns in to a grimace, and her voice is almost a growl as she answers, "I don't know why you are questioning how I got information. Elsie and I were talking in the lobby as we waited for all of our chapter members to assemble. Hattie and Myrtle had just joined us. Elsie got a call which seemed to shock her before she turned to me and said, 'My husband John just died.' She rushed into her apartment and closed the door. I sent you that text before we got on the elevator to come up here."

"I heard her too. I don't know which shocked me more, that her husband died or that she had a husband who was still alive without telling us," Myrtle says. I notice that she is wearing her favorite purple dress in contrast to her normal jeans and colorful long-sleeved shirts. I really should suggest that she stop wearing that dress. The grease spots down the front are now a continuous line of stain. Maybe I need to take her shopping. I think the news about Elsie has my mind wandering.

Hattie's wide brimmed red hat has bright teal ribbons that almost match the teal streaks she has added to the long sections of her hair. I never know what color she will try next. All of that teal blends well with the large flowers on her dress. Why do short, wide ladies want equally wide flowers on their dresses? Those ribbons seem to dance as she adds her own special touch to the conversation, "You know my hearing isn't what it used to be. I thought Elsie said she needed to go to the john. I couldn't figure out what that had to do with getting a phone call. I always have to go to the john, but that doesn't mean I rush off to do it after getting a phone call."

I try hard not to laugh, because it really isn't a laughing situation. Her voice has its normal tone that sounds like she just finished her fifth pack of cigarettes for the day. I wonder if she ever smoked or if it is from the second-hand smoke after her years as a bartender. Today will not be the day to ask her. I make a rapid decision, "Let me grab my purse and put on my shoes. We will continue with our lunch plans for now because it is too late to cancel on our other friends. Connie had sent a text that they were already waiting for us. Over lunch we can discuss how best to help Elsie. I will send her a text telling her where we have gone. She may need us before we return."

Once we reach our restaurant, we are quickly shown to the banquet room. I've never been sure whether that was out of courtesy or self-preservation as our group can normally be a little on the rowdy side. That is not the case today. There is the buzz of conversation as Betty, Hattie and Myrtle update everyone on Elsie. There are many expressions of shock and surprise. It seems that we were not the only ones who hadn't known about Elsie's husband. She has only lived in the St. James for about six months. That is usually more than enough time to learn the story of her life. Betty is delighted to tell everyone about how often she sees Elsie coming out of Mr. Johnson's apartment or how often he comes out of Elsie's. Hattie adds that that exchange often happens very early in the morning. Betty, Elsie, Hattie, and Mr. Johnson all have apartments on the first floor.

Our normal unspoken rule was that we do not discuss details of the relationship between Mr. Johnson and whichever of the residents he is dating. We could all guess who it is, because the current favorite will have a smile pasted on her face for weeks. Not a single woman appeared to be angry when their relationship ended, and he started a new one. He manages to make both current and past girlfriends feel special. Personally, I have resisted his flirtations. Some of the other women like to lead him on, but have not ever been involved. Myrtle startles me when she says, “My relationship with him didn’t last very long. He wanted me to come to his apartment, but I prefer to sleep in my own bed. He also wanted sex two to three times a week, and just once a week wore me out. That was wonderful when I was young and married to my first husband Paul. By the time I married my second husband, Harl, I was happy to just snuggle at night and occasionally have monthly sex.” I hear gasps coming from a number of the women. We were not raised to talk frankly about sex. To do so about sex with a man who is not your husband, is downright shocking.

I quickly shift the conversation to ways we could help Elsie.

Chapter Two

After a great deal of discussion over lunch, our group decides that only one of us should check in with Elsie. They are very swift to vote me into that job. Standing in front of Elsie's door, I realize I don't know what I should say. If I start with anything about her husband, I am stating loud and clear that we were gossiping about her. Out of the corner of my eye I see Betty peering out of her slightly open door. If I don't do this, I know she will. I take a deep breath before I knock. Elsie's face is chalky white with tears running down her cheeks, and her eyes red from crying. She puts her hand to her mouth to hold back a sob as I ask, "Elsie, how are you doing?" I put my arm around her shoulders to lead her back into her apartment. I close the door firmly behind us. Betty does not need to hear every word we say.

Elsie, like most of the women in our building, is what I would call a little bitty bird of a thing. I'm not sure she passes five feet and probably weighs less than 100 pounds. When we were girls, women were expected to make sure their men had plenty to eat, and we ate whatever was left. I'm not sure that is the reason my friends are so tiny, but it very well might be. I, on the other hand, stand 5'10" in my stocking feet. I was the oldest of five girls growing up on our farm. I was expected to work as hard as the hired men, and was fed accordingly. All of my sisters were equally tall. I know in school we intimidated many a boy who thought he could keep us in our place. My sisters are all gone now, and I truly miss them. That might be part of the reason I am so comfortable in this building filled with women. Looking at Elsie, I feel she could use a hug. I want to ensure that the hug is a gentle one. I don't want to crush her in trying to make her feel better. As she starts to sob in my arms, I wish I had changed out of my good dress. I also should have put a Kleenex in my pocket. I pat her gently on the back, and let her cry for a few minutes.

She finally steps back and grabs tissues from the box on the coffee table. "I'm so sorry. I can't seem to stop crying. I'm sure you've heard that my husband John just died. He seemed so healthy during my visit early this morning. I just can't understand why he's gone." She blows her nose, grabs another tissue, and wipes her eyes. "Oh, I'm being a terrible hostess. Please sit." She waves at the chair across from the sofa. It is one of those chairs that looks like an ordinary armchair, but turns out to be a hidden rocker. I am glad that I figured that out by grabbing the arm before I sit down. I've been thrown off balance trying to sit in one of those buggers once before. Elsie wraps herself in a blanket that had been sitting beside her on the sofa. It must be that she is cold from shock, because I do believe it's 85° in this living room. With it this warm, my tears-soaked dress should dry quickly.

I take a deep breath before I say, "I have heard that he died, but to be honest Elsie, I had no idea that you were married. All of the women in the building had either never married or are widows. Why didn't you tell us that your husband was still alive?"

"It was selfish of me. I spent so many years with my entire life wrapped around his dementia. When I had to put him in that nursing home, I needed some space to find myself again. I could visit him each day, but the other twenty-three hours in the day were mine. I have loved him, cared for him, and now I have to bury him. I'd like to think that the last six months while I lived here have prepared me for living without him."

I'm not sure if that will turn out to be true, but I don't know how to tell her that. Instead, I say, "Elsie, I know from experience that the next few days and weeks will be hard for you. We are here if you want or need our help." I reach out to pat her hand before showing myself out.

Hattie, Betty, and Myrtle are all waiting for me in the foyer. When they all start to talk at once, I put my finger up to my lips to hush them. I point at the elevator. Once we are all in, and I've hit the button for the fifth floor I say, "I didn't want Elsie to hear us talking about her."

"What did she say," Hattie asks, "about her husband?"

Before I can answer, the elevator doors open. Florence is waiting for us in the foyer on the fifth floor. "Come in, all of you. Let me make us a pot of tea, and get some of the cookies I baked yesterday before I tell you what little I know." The women settle around my table. Having space for that table was one of the things that attracted me to this apartment. I love that it is so much bigger than the one-bedroom unit I had looked at first. It is not easy to find a downtown apartment that is both updated and affordable. I think about Elsie as I arrange cups, the teapot, and the cookies. I hear the general buzz from the conversation my friends are having before I take my place at the table. That conversation changes from questions to expressions of understanding and sympathy when I share Elsie's statement about John's dementia and the nursing home. With the exception of Betty, it is a story many of us know all too well. I wonder if this is part of the behavior my friend Claire calls an instant party whenever we are all together. A party attitude keeps the sad thoughts at a distance. Today, however, is clearly not a party.

Chapter Three

I head out the door early the next morning to begin my daily walk. I start up the hill and then cross over to Mill Park. I love to listen to the birds chirping away from all the bushes that line the walkway. I have to come early before the traffic sounds drown out the birds. This is my favorite part of the day. I remember how Myrtle and I walked everywhere when we shared that first apartment. I should ask her to join me on more of my walks now. This morning, however, my thoughts are focused on Elsie. I know she needs our help, but I'm not sure of the best way to do that. I remember from experience that planning a funeral is a very difficult time.

I am shaken by the shouting that I hear as I enter the front door to the building. A young man is standing in front of Elsie's open door. His fists are clenched at his side as he continues to yell. "You are the reason my father is dead. It was your job to take care of him. Instead, you stuck him in that home, so you could come here to live the high life." Elsie seems to shrink with every word he shouts. "I don't believe for a second that he died of natural causes. I'm calling the police, so they can arrest you for murder."

I have heard more than enough. I march over and stand in front of Elsie, looking the young man directly in the eye. "I don't know who you are, but you need to leave now." I cross my arms in front of me as I glare at him, and then point to the door.

Hattie has come out of her apartment with her phone in hand. I hear her say, "Yes officer, the young man is threatening one of our residents. I'm afraid he may hurt us."

"Did you just call the cops on me? Let them come, because this dumb bitch needs to be arrested. I want to see her get what she deserves. She only married my father to get his money."

By now Mr. Johnson has joined us in the lobby. "Young man, I will have you arrested if you don't leave this very minute. You are trespassing." The threat in Mr. Johnson's voice surprises me. I have always assumed he was a lover not a fighter. I walk over to open the door as I hear the siren in the distance.

"I'll leave, but this won't be the last of it. You are an evil old woman, and I know what you did to my father. I will make you pay for it. I'll also make certain that you don't get any of his money." By now Elsie has collapsed to her knees crying. Hattie and Betty, both help her to her feet. I'll let Mr. Johnson deal with the police. I join my friends as we assist Elsie into her apartment.

Betty goes straight to the kitchen to fill the tea kettle. "I'll have tea ready in just a minute. That should help all of us to settle down quickly." Hattie and I take a seat on the couch with Elsie between us.

Hattie calls out, "Only if you add a shot of brandy, will having a cup of tea work for me." I don't say anything, but I do think that Hattie's got a point.

Elsie takes a few deep breaths. I'm happy to see that she has some color back in her cheeks. I was concerned about how pale she had gotten. She calls out, "Betty, turn off the teakettle. I think it's time I shared some facts with you. We should probably collect as many of the ladies as possible downstairs, so I don't have to repeat myself or worry about the misinterpretations in the building's gossip network. Send out the messages. Tell everyone to be downstairs in thirty minutes. I need a hot shower to wash off the grime from that boy. Please lock the door on your way out." I am surprised by her tone of resignation. I have a flash thought pop into my head. Surely, she isn't going to say that she murdered her husband?

Hattie and Betty look at me. I shrug and point toward the door. Once outside my two friends are busy deciding how to divide up the message groups. I send one to Mr. Johnson asking for the keys to the banquet room. He replies that he will meet us downstairs. I wonder if we need a secretary to keep notes for this meeting. I also wonder how Elsie will feel about including Mr. Johnson.

Chapter Four

Back in my own apartment, I fill a plate of cookies from my fresh batch of oatmeal raisin. If I had known we were going to have this gathering, I would have baked a second batch of chocolate chip. I have no idea just what Elsie wants to tell us. She has not been shy about how happy she has been since she started dating Mr. Johnson. Not all of our residents have been that open about their relationship with the man. He is tall, reasonably fit, with some silver hair, and as my daddy used to say, 'silver tongued.' He looks so much better since he stopped wearing that ugly black toupee. One of the women must have convinced him that natural silver is better than dyed black. I have to admit he is charming. Being the only man living in the building really doesn't hurt his chances for romance. I'm not looking for romance myself. I am much more impressed with the fact that he has the skills to keep the building in tip top shape. I am sure it is those skills that were important to Terry Thompson, owner of the building, when he hired Mr. Johnson. I also am sure that Mr. Johnson's selection of baby blue leisure suits was not a factor. None of the women have convinced him to change his wardrobe.

Terry had been as careful with the remodel of the banquet room as he had been with each of the units in the building. It has the same cream walls and white trim. The kitchen has the same granite countertops and new upscale stainless-steel appliances. There are three sinks similar to those found in commercial kitchens. The large island has a butcher block top with enough room for three or more cooks. The wrought iron pot rack has the large kettles and pans needed to feed a crowd. The 48-inch stove and oven is something I could use if I ever wanted to start selling my cookies. The two dishwashers make cleanup very easy.

Today the kitchen will only be used for making coffee and tea in the large urns.

The banquet room is often used for family gatherings that are too large for a one-bedroom apartment. We also use it for our holiday potlucks. Those gatherings are much more fun together than being locked away by ourselves to celebrate a holiday. The very best gathering, however, had been when Claire had married Terry. She had lived in the apartment next door to mine. Being in her fifty's, she had been such a delightful addition to our group of women. Terry and Claire held both the wedding and the reception here so all of the residents could attend. It was a beautiful wedding. It didn't hurt that having Claire's friends, their partners, and both sets of children attending meant there was more than two men to ask us to dance. Somehow, I don't think today's gathering will produce those same fond memories. Now Terry's mother, Florence, lives next door. I miss Claire, but Florence has been a longtime friend.

The ladies have organized chairs into two rows of a semi-circle. Elsie pulls a chair over to the opening of that semi-circle. Mr. Johnson takes a seat off to the backside of the group. Elsie glances at him before she clears her throat. Hattie has gotten up to retrieve the box of tissues from the counter that lines the wall. She gives Elsie's shoulder a quick squeeze as she sets the box on the floor beside Elsie's chair. Elsie looks down at her hands folded in her lap before she begins to speak in a very soft voice. Hattie calls out, "Honey, you're gonna have to speak up if you want us to hear you. Some of us just don't hear as well as we use to."

Elsie raises her head before she begins again. "As I'm sure you have all heard by now, my husband John was alive and living in a nursing home when I moved into this building. We had been married for fifteen years. He was semi-retired from his law practice when I met him. I was living in a tiny condo, and moved into his house after the wedding. The house was decorated by his late wife and still contained many of her personal things. I quickly learned how controlling he was when he informed me, I was not to change a thing. I knew I had made a mistake, but I had pledged to love, honor, and obey him. The addition of 'in sickness or in health' expanded that pledge less than four years later. By then he was clearly showing signs of dementia. There were moments when he realized things weren't right. He made me promise not to share his condition with his son and daughter. I had to trust that he could handle our financial resources. He never shared with me how much money he had or how it was to be spent. He often told me I would be well taken care of in his will. I don't have to have the will read to know that's not true. I won't go into details but the only thing I can count on is my spousal Social Security." Elsie takes a moment to wipe the tears from her eyes and blow her nose. I watch as she shreds the tissues in her lap. "I expect I will hear even more hatred from his son and possibly his daughter. Neither of them were happy when John and I married. Brett is as domineering with his wife Carol as John was with me. John's daughter Jane is a mousy little thing who married a man just like her father. It has taken me the last six months to see how much of myself I lost during those fifteen years of marriage. Even with dementia, John tried to control everything around me. I did my best while dealing with his almost bipolar behavior as the dementia took over more and more of his brain. I really don't want to talk about the years I spent caring for him. Those memories are just too painful. Thank you all for being my friends. I will let you know when and where I have his memorial."

Chapter Five

I find myself thinking about Elsie's years with John as I start my early walk the next morning. Her marriage was nothing like my marriage with George. He had been so supportive of everything I ever wanted to do. He encouraged me to have a job, to spend time with my friends, and to generally have a life that went beyond him. We were true partners as we raised our daughter. He also encouraged her to get an education, and to enjoy her accomplishments in addition to being a wife and mother. He's been gone for twenty years, but I still miss him. I doubt that Elsie would say that about John twenty years from now. I am glad that she has found some happiness with Mr. Johnson even if it is only for a few months. I do wonder if he knew she was still married when they started seeing each other.

I have no idea if Elsie is an early riser or what time she may return to her own apartment if she spent the night in Mr. Johnson's. Just the same, I knock on her door to see how she is doing. She actually smiles as she opens the door. I take that as a good sign. "Good morning, Elsie. I wanted to check on you. Is there anything I can do for you? Do you need help selecting a coffin or organizing the funeral? I remember how hard it was to make those decisions after my husband died."

"Thank you, Mabel; that is very kind of you. Please come in. I just made coffee, and I could use the company."

As I take a seat at the small bar between Elsie's kitchen and living room, I am again struck by how much smaller this apartment is than what my friends call my 'penthouse' unit. I say another thank you to George for having done such an excellent job at managing our retirement money. I am far from wealthy, but I am able to afford my rent and can even travel if I so wish. It might be time for my daughter and me to do that in the near future. I turn my thoughts back to Elsie as she hands me a cup and says, "Let's sit in the living room."

Taking a seat on the sofa I notice how sparsely the room is furnished. There is one small table with one lamp and that chair opposite the sofa that I sat in last time. Many of my friends have their living rooms crowded with furnishings. Elsie does not have pictures or even dried flower arrangements. I have to ask, "Besides John's children, do you have children of your own?"

Elsie seems to droop at my question. She sounds so sad as she answers, "I so wanted to have children, but it was not an option with my first husband. Someday when this is over, I'll have to tell you about that marriage. For now, making decisions about John will be relatively easy. He will be cremated and his urn buried beside his first wife. I didn't know her, but she is welcome to him for eternity. I will plan a brief grave side service in a week or so. I could use your help at finding a low-cost way to do that. More importantly, I really could use a friend to go with me when his will is read tomorrow. Would you do that? It won't be a pretty scene, but I know you would be strong enough to help me deal with it."

"If you want me there, of course I will join you." I remember her brief comment about the will yesterday. I wonder why she says reading of that will may not be pretty, but I can think about that tomorrow. I head back up to my apartment to bake a new batch of cookies. Somehow, I think we might need them. Mixing up cookies always helps me clear my mind.

Although many attorneys in King County have their offices in downtown Seattle close to the courthouse, I am amazed by the number of offices located in downtown Kent. Fortunately, Elsie and I only have to walk two blocks to reach her late husband's former office. Leaving the St.

James at 8 AM means that most of the residents won't notice that we have gone. Undoubtedly, the network will be in full force when we return. I decide it is best to chat about the weather and the flowers that are blooming along the way. I may have questions for Elsie after the visit to the attorney's office, but I don't need to add to her anxiety before we get there.

The attorney's office has that old money look with dark wood and burgundy leather furniture. The receptionist gives Elsie a sweet smile as she says, "Mrs. Hansen, it is good to see you again, but I am so sorry for your loss. Mr. Emery is waiting for you in his office."

"Thank you dear." We proceed down the hall to the open door where a silver haired older gentleman rises from behind his desk. Elsie extends her hand, "Mark, thank you for doing this so quickly. I'd like to introduce you to my friend Mabel Schmidel." Mark reaches out to grasps first Elsie's hand and then mine. I am struck by how handsome he is. His hands wrap around mine with both warmth and a shot of electricity. He finally waves his hand toward the chairs to the right of his desk as she and I take seats. On the left side is the young man I recognize as her stepson. Beside him is a slightly older man who looks rumpled and clearly has a pouch hanging over his belt. Beside him is a woman who matches Elsie's description of a mouse. Her hair is a messy blonde mop that hides her face as she looks at her hands in her lap. I assume this is Elsie's stepdaughter, Jane Spencer. None of the men even look in Elsie's direction.

Elsie reaches out to take my hand as soon as Mark says, "Let's begin."

Chapter Six

Mark's voice has that deep baritone that I associate with TV judges. There is confidence and formality in the way he enunciates each word as he reads. The will starts with the normal 'last will and sound mind' verbiage I remember from the wills George and I had written. It continues with his desire to be cremated and to have his urn buried beside his first wife. Next, he bequeaths the house and all of its furnishings to Elsie along with his life insurance policy. The following part surprises me. Because his son and daughter have not been kind to Elsie, he leaves them each the grand total of $1,000. I hear the children gasp. Mark continues despite the whispering that can be heard between Brett and Jane's husband, Don. Jane has yet to even look up at the attorney. The last item is that any funds remaining in his retirement account are to be given to the Xavier Onward Christian Ministry. As Mark closes the file on his desk, Brett and Don are on their feet to express their outrage.

Both Brett and Don are shouting at the top of their lungs. Brett is practically screaming, "My father would never do this to us. That woman has stolen our inheritance. We will contest this will. She has already sold that house and everything in it." Don chimes in, "We demand she return that money." They continue to yell at Mark and Elsie as she and I turn to leave the room. Mark turns slightly to nod his head in our direction.

The last thing I hear before I close the door behind us is Mark saying, "Contesting the will is your right. I will tell you that your father and I drafted this will two years after he married Elsie. Although his dementia worsened in later years, he knew exactly what he was doing when he drafted it."

Elsie is very quiet as we walk back to the St. James. Once we arrive, she surprises me when she asks, "May I come upstairs with you? I have a couple of things I want you to know. I feel I can trust you not to share all of this with the other residents."

Once we are in my apartment, I head straight to the kitchen. I put the plate of cookies on the table as Elsie takes a seat there. "Can I offer you coffee, tea, a glass of milk, or a stiff drink?"

Elsie gives me a weak smile, "The stiff drink is tempting, but probably not a good idea. Coffee would undoubtedly make me more jittery than I already feel, so let's go for tea." She reaches for a napkin and a cookie. I add two cups to the table and then the teapot once the water is hot. As much as I would like to jump in with questions, I decide it is best if I wait until Elsie is ready. "I didn't know about the thousand dollars to each of the children. John did tell me how angry he was over the way they treated me from the day of our wedding. What they don't know is that the estate has no way of paying them even that small amount."

"Surely you have money from the sale of the house? Wouldn't it be the civil thing to at least honor that bequest?"

Even that weak smile has faded as Elsie answers me, "John's dementia had progressed to the point that a year ago I had to take control of our finances. I realized how bad things were when I got the notice that our electric was about to be shut off. Until that time, he had insisted on paying all of the bills for the house because it was his house. My Social Security went to buy food and cover any medical bills. I soon learned that not only had he not paid the electric, but he had failed to pay the water and sewer bills or the taxes. There was no extra money in our bank account. I had to start selling the furniture to get the utilities and taxes up to date. That was really only the beginning.

There was no money left in his retirement account; he had drawn it all out and sent most of it to that online ministry. In addition, he had mortgaged the house, and failed to make the mortgage payments. I assume that money also went to the same place. I managed to get the house sold before the foreclosure action started because Mark had helped me with a power of attorney the year before. What little was left went for his care in that nursing home. I didn't tell Brett and Jane because I didn't want them to think badly of their father. By the time I moved here, I was just exhausted."

I am shocked. Over the last few years many of the women have shared their tales about being left with poverty income. That had been one of Terry's considerations when he set the rent. Elsie's situation, however, is the worst I have ever heard. I reach across the table to squeeze her hand, "I had no idea. That must have been so hard. Do you think the children will try to contest the will?"

"Mark understands the status of the estate. I'm sure he will find a way to deflect their efforts. I've done all I can to protect them and John's memory."

Chapter Seven

It is time for me to send out the invitations to our bimonthly poker game at my place. Although there are two of our residents who do not like to play poker, I try to make certain that everyone gets at least an every-other month invitation even if they aren't able or willing to attend. I usually keep the party invitation number between six and seven of the women. We always have a good time even though the games can get quite competitive. We like to say we play for high stakes even if those stakes are pieces of wrapped candy. Currently peppermint is a five-dollar bet and butterscotch is a ten which is our table limit. All soft chewy candy has been rejected for being too hard on dental work.

The difficult part about deciding on the guest list is to make certain I have excluded Mr. Johnson's current favorite. I could never claim that we didn't gossip. We may be little old ladies, but no one ever said that we were "sweet" little old ladies. Maybe that's the reason we gamble with candy. The challenge has been knowing who that favorite might be. Who knew that a man could be traded back and forth like small boys do with baseball cards? My instincts say that Elsie would benefit from the friendly diversion of the poker game. I can't invite her, however, because her relationship with Mr. Johnson seems to still be going strong. I don't know exactly when it started, but it has been going for approximately three months which is almost a record.

Even if Elsie was not the current favorite, there is no way around the fact that she will be the hot topic. I finalize the list with Florence, Hattie, Betty, Myrtle, Ethel and myself. With luck, Ethel or Myrtle will share stories about new adventures with their boyfriends. That always livens up the poker game.

The game starts off with the ante of one peppermint and sips from the mugs filled with my signature mulled wine. Each of the women try to glance at the others around the table without appearing to look. The hope is the we can read the expression on the faces of the others to be able to guess what kind of hand we each have. The goal is to glean that information without giving away anything about our own hand. You would think we were playing in a professional poker tournament. Myrtle raises the ante another peppermint and asks the question that is also been on my mind, "Has Elsie said anything about her husband's funeral?"

"She told me that she plans to have a grave side service next week. She said he wanted to be cremated, but hasn't said that that has been done. I don't understand what may be causing that delay."

Ethel looks like the cat that swallowed the canary as she says, "As you know my friend Clem's son is a police detective. Clem told me that her stepson called the department to demand an autopsy. He is convinced Elsie murdered her husband!" This is not what I was expecting when I thought Ethel might add spice to the poker game.

The poker party goes downhill from there. For Elsie's sake, I can only hope that the allegation is proven to be false.

Two days later I am trying to decide whether I want to bake chocolate chip or peanut butter cookies. Both are favorites with my friends. I assume that we will be spending part of the day helping Elsie plan the service. The funeral home must have done the cremation by now. As I am turning on the oven to preheat, my phone rings. Before I can even say hello, I hear Betty shouting into the phone, "Mabel, you need to get down here fast. The police are knocking on Elsie's door, and I know Mr. Johnson is still in there. This may get ugly quickly. We need your help." I am on my way to the elevator before she even finishes the call.

The scene before me is reminiscent of the one from last week. Elsie's door is open and Mr. Johnson is in front of her facing a man that I instantly recognize. Stan Mason was one of the detectives who had investigated the murder of Claire's first husband. We had all called him the nasty one. A man that I did not recognize stood next to him. I assume he is Stan's new partner. I hear him say, "Mrs. Hansen, we really only want to ask you a few questions about your late husband."

Mr. Johnson holds his arms out to block the doorway. He says, "Elsie, you don't have to talk to them. Just step back and close your door. I'll deal with them." Stan takes another step forward. Mr. Johnson raises his fist and swings in an effort to hit Stan. In a flash, Stan has Mr. Johnson pressed against the wall while his partner snaps on handcuffs.

Elsie crumples to the floor as she says, "Oh Zeb, what have you done now?" Stan reaches out to take Elsie's elbow as he helps her to her feet. My instinct is to march over and make sure she is okay. I must have made a noise, because Stan turns toward me. "Mrs. Schmidel, please stay where you are." He reaches behind Elsie to close her door. "Mrs. Hansen, you need to come with me to the station." He leads her toward the front door following his partner who has taken Mr. Johnson.

Betty looks at me with a look of shock on her face. "Mabel, you're going to need to have Florence call Terry. I think Mr. Johnson will need a lawyer. Elsie may need one as well."

Before I can answer, Diana Sullivan steps out from behind me. "Mabel, if you can drive me, I can act as Elsie's attorney. I may have retired from my law practice, but I am still a licensed attorney. I do hope that she doesn't say anything while she's in the car." For the first time I'm truly afraid for Elsie. Will Diana be able to save her from herself? And what do we do about saving Mr. Johnson?

Chapter Eight

I have always thought that Diana was a striking woman. She is a little shorter than I am, but now wearing heels she has to be close to 6 foot tall. Where I tend to be very curvy as a full-figured woman, she is slim with an athletic build and almost military posture. Her bright white shirt highlights her short-cropped snow-white hair with curls wrapping around her face. Her dark skin adds a glow to her black suit in a way that makes it almost an extension of her body. As she strides toward me, I think of an African warrior like those I remember from the pages of National Geographic when I was a girl. I am smart enough not to share a comment about that image. I'm afraid such a comment might be considered racist instead of the highlighting the admiration that I feel. I do say, "You look like you are ready to do battle."

Diana laughs. The sound rings almost like a wind chime in a strong breeze. "Thank you. Let's hope the police feel the same way. I'm afraid Elsie may be in more trouble than she realizes." She continues as I lead the way to my car. "Thank you also for driving. In my former life I always took taxis. This should help us get to the police station much faster."

"I'm still amazed that you could go from jeans and sweatshirt to a full set of attorney armor in five minutes. I'm proud to be your sidekick. Let's go save Elsie."

I consider it a good omen to easily find a parking space in the lot across from the police station. I pat myself on the back for being able to keep up with Diana's long strides. Once inside the front doors, she waves me to a seat in what is clearly their waiting area. She continues to the counter where she is greeted by a woman sitting behind a glass panel. Her voice takes on a sharp edge of authority as she says, "I am Diana Sullivan. I am here to see my client, Elsie Hansen who I believe has been brought in for questioning." The door beside the counter is opened by an officer. Diana strides through without a backward glance.

This chair is hard. Why do so many waiting areas have extremely uncomfortable seating? I imagine that here they want you to understand that their work is serious. Or maybe they want you to do penance for being a lawbreaker. That might not be the case, because the chairs in my doctor's office are equally uncomfortable. I can't dream that the doctor's office wants you to do penance for being sick. A friend once told me that restaurant chairs were specifically designed to have you only partially comfortable while you have your meal and then dessert. After that they want the chair to tell you it is time to leave so new diners can be seated. I have let my mind wander as I try not to think about what is happening with Elsie and Diana. As the minutes tick by I am reminded of how unprepared I am to sit and wait. I did not bring the book I am reading, nor am I one of those little old ladies who keeps her knitting in her purse. I check my phone, but there is nothing except a text from Betty asking about Elsie. I don't reply because I have nothing to report.

About thirty minutes later a man in a suit comes in the outer door followed by Terry Thompson. Is this an attorney for Mr. Johnson? Terry sighs as he takes the seat beside me and pats my hand. The other man proceeds to the counter just as Diana had done. "I am Ken Smith, attorney for Zebadiah Johnson. I need to see my client." The door is opened and he too disappears from sight.

Terry turns to look squarely at me. "So, Mabel, fill me in on what is happening at the St. James that has you and me sitting together in the police station lobby."

Do I give him the short version or the longer one that hopefully I won't be able to finish before we get out of here? I don't know Terry that well, but somehow I'll bet that the short version will lead to more questions. I take a deep breath and start my story. Watching the frown on his face become more firmly fixed, I worry that he may decide to evict Elsie from the building and/or fire Mr. Johnson. I don't want either of those things to happen. Elsie needs our support, and besides doing a good maintenance job, Mr. Johnson adds a level of fun to our day-to-day lives. As I finish my update, I decide that I really need to stand up. I've been in that chair for just under two hours and my body is stiff. My butt is downright numb. Maybe I should have done this earlier, because the door opens for Elsie and Diana to exit followed closely behind by Mr. Johnson and Mr. Smith. Diana takes Elsie's elbow, and I hear her whisper in Elsie's ear, "Don't say anything to anyone until we are outside and in the car."

As we reach the door, I hear Terry say, "Thank you Ken. I will take him home. We can all talk later." Outside in the parking lot, I see Terry fold his arms across his chest as he says to Mr. Johnson, "Zeb, what were you thinking?" Somehow, I think that is the point; I honestly don't think Mr. Johnson was thinking, but rather just reacting. I know he was trying to protect Elsie, but I just can't picture him in that same warrior pose that I can for Diana. I do hope that she is able to give Elsie the protection she clearly needs.

Chapter Nine

Elsie blows her nose after climbing into the back seat of my car. I can hear that she is still crying. I dare not look at her, or I will be crying as well. Diana manages to look graceful as she folds her long legs into the front seat. I give her a quick glance before I carefully pull out of the parking lot. She turns to Elsie before she asks, “Do I have your permission to share part of what we learned, with Mabel?”

“Please, because I can’t.” Elsie blows her nose again.

“Because John’s son insists that Elsie murdered John, the police ordered an autopsy. It shows that he may have been smothered. The time of death is estimated to be shortly after Elsie signed out on the visitor log. No one else had signed in as a visitor to John, although other people signed in to visit residents of that wing. Those sign-ins were all a full hour after Elsie had already left. As of now she is the prime suspect, but they have no concrete evidence to link her to John’s death. I have no doubt that they will be trying to find that evidence. This will probably be only the first round of their questions. Stan Mason strikes me as a very thorough detective. He is definitely not one I would consider personable.”

This does not sound good for Elsie, but I don’t want to say that out loud. She is clearly suffering more than enough right now. Instead, I say, “I agree about Stan Mason. I remember him oh too well when he was part of the investigation of Claire Murphy Thompson’s late husband. What do we do now?”

“For now, it is a matter of wait and see. We go back home where I get to change into my comfortable jeans and take off these damn heels. We may wish to call another all-building meeting. It will not help Elsie to have rumors floating in all directions." She gives me a tentative smile.

"What about Mr. Johnson? Did they actually arrest him? Will he have to go to court?"

"I was only there to represent Elsie. I will call Ken once I get to my apartment. I may or may not be able to share any information with you after I make that call. Because Terry was able to drive him home, I assume he was not charged."

Oh, how I wish I could make all of this okay instantly.

I send a group text to my close friends to meet in the banquet room in an hour. They will make certain that it is forwarded to all of the residents. I'm sure I only need to send it to Betty. One of these days I'll do that, and then set a timer to see exactly how long it takes before it comes back to me after everyone else has seen it. Elsie replies that she won't be there. She says she intends to take a nap. I suspect that she does not feel up to facing everyone. Mr. Johnson also says he won't be there, but that I can pick up the key from him beforehand. I wonder if he is also not up to facing all of the residents. I fill a plate with cookies before heading downstairs early. I want to have coffee and tea ready before everyone arrives.

The room fills slowly as the ladies enter in small groups. Although we are all friendly, there are distinctive groups that are closer than others. I won't go so far as to call them cliques, but even the colors they decide to wear show their set membership. Some of the women wear bright colors and lipstick to match. Others tend more toward very feminine pastels. Personalities match those color selections. The network has spread with the reason for the meeting. This is clearly not a party. I have known some of these women for most of my life. Others I've only met while living here in the St. James. They have all become my friends. Like any group of women, there can be bickering, gossiping, or jealousy. I had remarked as I started into menopause, that my body felt like it did when I was twelve and just starting to have my periods. Now, in the last quarter of our lives, we act more like high school girls. I doubt if any of us are up to trying out for the cheerleading squad, but happily there has been no hair pulling over the affections of Mr. Johnson.

Diana may have changed into jeans to go with that white shirt, but she still strides into the room like she is ready to do battle. Her voice has that same air of authority as she calls out, "Ladies, if I can have your attention. This really won't take very long. As you know by now, Elsie and Mr. Johnson had been taken to the police station for questioning. The police believe that Elsie's late husband may have been smothered. At this time there is no doubt in my mind, that Elsie is their prime suspect. Because of Mr. Johnson's actions, he also becomes a suspect. The allegations that started this investigation were made by her husband's son. Over the next few days, the police will be here often, and will want to question each of you. As Elsie's attorney, there is very little that I can say to them. For all of you, I want you to remember a couple of things. Number one, tell them the truth, and nothing but the truth." All of us are old enough to remember when Joe Friday said those words regularly on that TV show. I see a few shy smiles as members of one of the groups of women visibly relax just a bit. Diana continues, "Number two, answer only the questions that you are asked. Do not volunteer information that is not asked for. Number three, do not answer with any gossip. If you do not know the answer in your own personal experience, say you don't know. To do anything else may put Elsie and Mr. Johnson in greater peril than they are already."

Betty is the first to speak, "Does this mean, I have to tell them that I have seen Mr. Johnson leaving Elsie's apartment early in the morning?"

"Only if they ask that question specifically. Remember, you do not know just why Mr. Johnson may have been there early in the morning. Unless one of the two of them has told you direct details about their relationship, you do not know what goes on behind those closed doors. Are there any more questions?"

Not a whisper comes from any of the women in the room. I use my best imitation of Betty's teacher voice, "Elsie should be able to continue with her plans for the service the first of next week. I will let you know the details once they have been confirmed. I hope all of you will plan to attend, because I really think she needs our support." The silence continues as the groups of women file out of the banquet room.

Chapter Ten

Betty, Hattie, and Myrtle follow me to my apartment. Ethel and Florence join us a few minutes later. Everyone silently takes a seat at my table. I put the teakettle on, although my first instinct is to go with something stronger. Ethel kicks things off when she says, "I'm afraid that Elsie and Mr. Johnson are going to need our help. How can her stepson be that nasty?"

"I'm sure that it is hard for grown children to see their parent with a new love. Remember how Claire's friend Megan struggled with the hatred from Richard Olson's children? When he died, it got even worse. I think that was part of the reason Megan moved to Galveston," Florence says. "Terry and Claire have been very lucky, because both sets of their children seem to be happy as a blended family."

Betty asks, "How do we even begin to help? I've never experienced the death of a husband, let alone one who was murdered."

Ethel addresses the elephant in the room. "We don't really think that Elsie or Mr. Johnson could have murdered her husband, do we?"

The women look at each other before shaking their heads 'No.' I take a deep breath before I answer for the group, "I can't see that either of them could do such a thing. I think we need to help by finding better suspects."

A big smile spreads across Hattie's face, "Maybe we need to start with binge watching murder movies. Where did Sam Spade start with his investigations?"

"We might qualify for the role of Miss Marple," Betty says with a chuckle "I just don't see that Agatha Christie would do us much good. I never know who the villain is until Hercule Poirot gathers them all together. Even then I have to wait until he points out the bad guy."

Ethel says, "The shows I watch all start with a whiteboard. We could list the suspects, and what we know about each of them."

I shake my head, "That is probably a good idea, but we clearly didn't know enough about Elsie before the death of her husband. How do we go about learning more?"

Florence cocks her head to the side and gives me a very serious look. "If we are going to become detectives, we probably need to know what strengths we each bring to the table. Do we need a second whiteboard to list all of us and the areas where we can do the research?"

"I'm not expecting to have overnight guests in the near future. We could put up paper on the walls in my guestroom."

Betty almost bounces in her seat as she says, "We could use colored markers to highlight different facts. When I taught, I only had old fashioned blackboards. We weren't allowed to use colored chalk because it was too hard for the janitor to clean it off."

"Colored markers might bleed through paper onto your walls. I can ask Terry if he has an extra whiteboard or two. I know he keeps a number of them in his construction trailer. He might just have extras we can borrow."

Hattie nods her head, "I'm going shopping later today. I will pick up colored whiteboard markers. We can label one board, Suspects and the second one Detectives. We may need a name for ourselves. 'The #1 Ladies Detective Agency'© has already been used. Maybe we should call ourselves the St. James Lady Detectives."

"It might be a bit early to address ourselves as detectives. Let's plan to meet back here tomorrow morning about nine. At the very least we can use paper and pencils to list what we know. Diana may have additional information by then as well."

Not even the sound of the birds can help put my mind at ease during my morning walk. How can a group of old women help Elsie, if she really is in as much trouble as Diana has implied? To help her, we will need to break another of the St. James building unspoken rules. We will need to ask her about all aspects of her life before coming to the St. James. The rule allows each woman to share as much or as little of her past life as she wants. During some of our building's poker parties, members have shared stories about how they met their husbands, or how the love of their life got away. Sharing those stories has always been voluntary. Not everyone wants to do so. How do we even begin to ask Elsie? Should I plan an informal gathering with the intent of sharing some of those stories? If I do so, will Elsie decide to share? Right now, I think she is still in so much shock that she wouldn't feel the need to voluntarily share. Like it or not one of us is going to have to ask her. That does not need to be today. For now, we can list the things we know, and the questions we think need answers. It is time for us to get started.

Chapter Eleven

I am just returning from my walk as Terry joins me at the front door. He has at least one whiteboard tucked under his arm. "Good morning, Terry. As always, it's delightful to have you here. I see that your mother called you about the whiteboards."

"She did, so I have two boards to drop off to you. I'm not sure what you ladies are up to, but I will trust that it is not something that may put you in danger."

I decide it is safer to just smile at him as the elevator delivers us to the fifth floor. "You can place those on the bed in my guestroom. Thank you so much. I'll let you know when we are done with them."

"Claire did say that you are to call her, if she can help you with your project."

"Give that darling girl my love." I start to breathe again after leaning against my closed-door. I hadn't thought we might be putting ourselves in any danger with our attempts to help Elsie. I trust that neither she nor Mr. Johnson could have harmed Elsie's late husband. Even after saying that to myself, I suddenly have the desire for a stiff drink. I will settle for finding the perfect place to park the whiteboards.

My friends are almost subdued as they file in to my apartment. They each take a seat at the table. Betty reaches for the package of colored markers that Hattie has removed from the bag. "Why do they package everything with that damn hard plastic that requires a knife just to open it? Makes me want to put that knife to better use than just opening a package."

"I know just how you feel," Hattie says. She pulls a knife out of her pocket. "I brought my pocket knife. I didn't want to open the package at my place. I was afraid I would lose one of the markers."

Betty quickly selects the blue marker that is almost a perfect match for her hair today, and then reaches for one of the whiteboards I have laying in the middle of the table. I try not to cringe as she slides the board toward her. My table may be old, but I really didn't want another scratch. Oh well, I'll worry about that later. Betty writes Detectives at the very top and then adds our names in a list below. A quick glance shows that she has placed us in alphabetical order. She puts the cap on that marker before picking up the black one. She puts Diana's name at the very bottom in black. She announces, "You will each need to add what single trait you have that will help us as detectives. I expect you to each use a different color. I'll start with the black and Diana as the law. I will also use black, and my trait is organization. I'll keep notes of everything we learn." That is clearly one thing that we have all come to expect from Betty. She passes the board to Hattie.

Hattie picks up the orange marker. Like Betty, the color is a match for her, as it is matching the orange flowered leggings she is wearing. The color is a sharp contrast to her bright red tee shirt. All of this contrasts with her hot pink hair. She looks very serious as she says, "Gossip. As a former bartender, I quickly learned how to get people to share the gossip they have heard. Gossip usually has an element of truth. Elsie said John had been an attorney, so I can also visit his office, and see if I can get anyone there to talk. I'm certain the staff knows more than they will share with the police. I will go to the area bars. There is sure to be a favorite the office staff frequent. Bartenders hear everything." She writes gossip on the board and passes it to Ethel.

Ethel looks slightly peevish as she faces Hattie, and then looks back at the board with the brown marker in her hand. "I was going to say I could contribute gossip. Now I have to think of a new term to write. You all know about my friend Clem. His son is Stan Mason's new partner."

This statement instantly causes a stir. I could hear the surprise from the women as they say, "That could be useful. Do you think he'll share facts about the case? How do we get him to help us?"

I also hear Hattie say, "Did she say that Stan Mason is her partner? Surely Ethel wouldn't trade Clem for Stan Mason. Clem is such a sweet man. Stan Mason is just nasty."

Ethel looks directly at Hattie and raises her voice slightly, "Hattie, you really need to get hearing aids. I said that Clem's son, Dean Swanson is Stan Mason's new partner. Since I can't use the word 'gossip 'I will settled for 'police insider.' I'll do my best to get Clem to ask questions of his son. I'm just not sure how much Dean will be able to share." She hands the whiteboard to Myrtle.

"I was also going to say gossip," says Myrtle. "My Elmer still goes to the fruit stand every day. He is been in business since he was sixteen. I think he knows everybody in South King County. I'll bet he knew Elsie's husband John. I can ask him what he knows about John's business." She writes business on the board with a yellow marker and passes the board to Florence.

"I was my late husband's bookkeeper. The detective shows all say follow the money. I'm not sure yet whose money I need to follow, but I can crunch the numbers once we have them." She uses the green marker to add $$ signs after her name. "I also still have my car, and can drive anyone if they can't take the bus. Mabel, it is your turn." She hands me the board and I select the pink marker.

"Before I turned to cookies, I had been a nurse. I can talk to the staff at John's nursing home. I'll also see if I can learn anything after a visit to the city morgue. Like Florence, you all know I have my car. You can call me if you need a ride. Do we want to wait to start our list of suspects until all of us have had a chance to start our investigations?"

Florence is the first to answer, "I agree that we need to collect more information before we turn to suspects. I'm afraid I'm like the police. Right now, my only suspect is Elsie, and I don't even want to consider that." The rest of the women all nod their heads in agreement.

Before taking her teacup to the kitchen, Hattie says in a loud voice, "I still think we need a name for ourselves. I expect everyone to have a suggestion before we meet again. Let's give ourselves two days to see what we can learn. Betty, you may need to bring a tape recorder next time. You will want to make certain that the notes you keep actually reflect what we've said." I try not to smile considering how Hattie is the one who has difficulty in hearing things correctly. With Hattie's statement, the ladies all quietly head out my door with looks of determination on their faces.

Chapter Twelve

As I clean up the teacups and put away the last of the cookies, it dawns on me that I need a lot more information from Elsie. I hate to disturb her, but I don't see any way around it. I don't even know the name of the nursing home that John lived in. I take some of the cookies out of the cookie jar and place them in a Tupperware container to take with me. I truly hope Mr. Johnson isn't there, but I don't want to call ahead. Maybe I should ask Florence to go with me. I make that call, and five minutes later the two of us are standing in front of Elsie's door. As I knock, I see Betty's door open slightly. The network will be in full force.

Elsie still looks pale and has now added dark circles under her eyes. As I give her a hug, I note the faint smell of an unwashed old lady body. It is still before noon, but I do wonder if she is taking care of herself. I'll add that to the questions I need to ask. Florence raises her eyebrows as she looks at me over Elsie's shoulder while she gives Elsie a hug. I'm afraid she has also noted the aroma. Florence steps back and places both hands on Elsie's shoulders. She looks Elsie straight in the eye as she asks, "Dear, are you taking good care of yourself?"

Elsie gives a negative shake to her head before waving us into the apartment. The whole room has the unwashed body smell. "I haven't been able to sleep. I just keep picturing John in a cardboard box as he is rolled into that furnace. Why did he want to be cremated? He always hated hot days." By now Elsie is sobbing. "They did the autopsy, but still haven't released John's body. I just want this to be over."

She is so upset that I don't know how we can possibly ask her questions. I think we need to try a different tactic. "Elsie, I can't make you sleep, but maybe you'll feel better after a good meal. Why don't you go take a hot shower and Florence and I'll be back to take you to lunch. Can you be ready in say forty-five minutes?" She blows her nose and nods her head yes. "Florence and I will pick you up. We can walk to that Italian restaurant we all love. I'll bet that a bowl of their soup and a salad will make you feel better." As Florence and I take the elevator back to the fifth floor, I have to say, "And I'm hoping that fresh air will get that awful smell out of my nose."

Florence adds, "I agree. Promise me that if I ever get that way, you will call Terry to have him put me in a home. If the police see her today, they will think she is falling apart from guilt. That may be true, but I don't think it is because she killed him. This strikes me as survivor guilt. I've seen it before from friends who don't understand why they didn't go first."

"I had forgotten those feelings. The heart attack took George so quickly. He was five years older, but I never considered that he would die first. I did feel guilty for just being alive. I can't imagine the guilt that Elsie must be feeling. Maybe after our lunch, I'll need to have a sit down with Diana. She may have some advice, but at the very least she needs to be aware of Elsie's state of mind. Now I need another shower to wash away that smell and a hot cup of tea to prepare me for this lunch."

One of the things I love about the St. James Apartments is the easy access to downtown Kent. Today we only need to go over the railroad tracks and then walk two more blocks to reach the Italian restaurant. The fresh air and the exercise seem to calm Elsie. My shower and cup of tea has done the same thing for me. As we open the door to the restaurant, we are wrapped in the aroma of garlic and Italian seasonings. My stomach instantly growls in response to these wonderful smells. The three of us agree that the minestrone soup with a salad sounds delightful. It only takes a couple of minutes before our salads are in front of us. Elsie takes a bite of hers before she turns her attention first to Florence and then to me. "Thank you for being my friends. I didn't realize how much I needed a shower, fresh air, and now food. I have just been wallowing in self-pity."

"You have been through a lot this week. I know when my husband George died, I just wanted to wrap myself up in a blanket and cry. I didn't give a damn about the outside world. After a week, my daughter showed up to take me to lunch just like we have with you. I know I felt guilty about outliving George. I am guessing you feel that way as well as thinking you should have done more. You did everything you could. Can you think of anyone who would have wanted to hurt John?"

"I have thought about this a lot. I honestly can't believe that it might have been one of his former clients. He hadn't been seeing clients in years, so I just can't see that as an option. Everyone at the Care Center had been so kind to both John and me. Nice people don't murder people in their care. I considered people outside those groups. I've never met anyone from the Xavier Onward Christian Ministry. I assume that they might have been upset when he stopped sending them money. Unless they knew about his will, I can't understand how his death would be to their advantage. I also feel guilty because the only person I can think of who might have done this, is his son. I could see that my stepson might have wanted to kill me, but not his own father. His father had been giving him money whenever he asked. John could no longer do this once I put him in the Care Center. Did Brett think I was hiding money? I didn't tell Brett or his sister Jane how much money had gone to pay off the mortgage and the cost of the Care Center. Maybe I should have shared that information? If he did do this, I just don't know how I could prove it."

Florence reaches out to pat Elsie's hand, "That's what your friends are for. Let's go back to my apartment where we can start collecting the details. I'm afraid that we will need to do our own investigation. I don't think we can trust this to just the police." I'm glad Florence suggested her apartment. I really don't want to answer Elsie's questions if she saw our white boards. We aren't gossiping behind her back, but I don't want to hurt her feelings. She has been through so much already.

Chapter Thirteen

I send out texts to all members of our investigative committee outlining the information Florence and I had gotten from Elsie. Tomorrow we will spread out to see what we can learn from the Care Center, John's law office, bank statements from all of Elsie and John's old accounts, and even some of the businesses in the area. I also plan to start my day at the morgue. Diana will meet with us the following day to review our results. I don't know whether to be excited or terrified by our efforts.

I had been a nurse for most of my life. I love the years I spent working alongside George in his practice. It had given me a sense of purpose, and a connection with him that ran deep. When he died, I didn't feel comfortable continuing despite my affection for all of his patients. I turned to a hospital setting which was much more fast paced. I missed the long-term relationships that I had formed with our patients. Instead, the patients moved so quickly through my wards I only had time to learn their names and medical details. The team of nurses and doctors that I worked with gave me a sense of belonging. Even the hospital smells became part of my normal workday. I can honestly say that the morgue only faintly has those same smells. The only reason I am here is for any information I might be able to glean from one of George's old friends, Duffy Fitzpatrick, the King County Medical Examiner. Duffy and George had far too many running bad jokes about Duffy needing to certify whenever one of George's patients died. Duffy was 30 years younger than George, but it didn't seem to ever be an issue with their friendship. We often had Duffy and his wife to our house for dinner. I hadn't stayed in touch as I should have. I'll use that as a reason for just dropping in, but I'll say that I had had an appointment at the medical center just across the street.

The young man manning the front desk looks more like a police officer than a receptionist. It dawns on me that things have changed a lot in the past few years. Although the death certificates are no longer stored here, this is an area that requires security. The glass window and door make me wonder if I'll even be able to speak with Duffy. Oh well, I'm here so I need to try. "Hi, I'm Mable Schmidel, Mrs. George Schmidel. I hoped to speak with Dr. Fitzpatrick who was a friend of my husband's. Is he available?"

"Please take a seat. I will call him." The young man was neither rude nor friendly. I guess I would say he was professional. I miss the days when a receptionist was warm and friendly. He actually turns away from me as he makes the call. He just nods at me as he hangs up the phone. I have no idea what that nod means until I see Duffy striding in my direction.

His white coat flaps around him as he comes into the small waiting area. "Mable, Dear, it has been much too long! What brings you here?"

Duffy seems to have aged a great deal in these few years, but the kindness in his eyes hasn't changed a bit. I feel tears forming, that I quickly bat away. "I am sorry to just drop in on you, but I was across the street for an appointment, and could not let more time pass without greeting you. Do you have a few moments to catch up?"

"I'll make some time. Give me about five minutes to wrap up a few things. There is a coffee shop just around the corner on 9th Avenue. Could you order me a latte and a sweet roll, any kind? That will give us more time to chat. I'm delighted that you dropped in. See you in a few."

If I didn't know Duffy as well as I did, I'd think I'd just gotten a brush off. Like George, I'm sure he is very careful about mixing his personal and professional lives.

I'm about to push that boundary. I hope it doesn't end what tenuous friendship that has remained.

"Hmm, I love the smell of fresh coffee. Thank you for doing the ordering. Thank you as well for the break in my work day. We've been far more busy than I really like. There have been more attacks on the homeless camps. Shameful. But you didn't stop to hear me moan about my work. I do apologize that we haven't stayed in touch as we should. Holiday cards just aren't enough. I did take note that you had sold the house a few years back. Where are you living now??

"I moved to Kent. The St James Apartments is now home. I miss my garden, but the building is filled with older women so I have companionship for this part of my life."

"I sense that there is more to this visit than just renewed friendship. Please tell me that none of your friends died a suspicious death?"

"No, but the husband of one of our residents died in Senior Services Care. We didn't even know that she was still married. Now the police think the man was murdered."

"How can I help?"

"I know you can't let me have a copy of the autopsy, but maybe you can help me understand how you determine murder?"

"We don't use the term 'murder' but rather 'homicide'. Sometimes there are direct signs; other times more invisible ones through blood tests or internal wounds. Your friend can request a copy of our report. She can then share it with anyone she wants. After she shares it with you, I will be happy to explain any questions she has. Who is the deceased so I will know to take her call personally rather than one of my assistants?"

"John Hansen. Elsie Hansen has lived in our building for the last six months. None of us think she could have been involved."

"Unfortunately, our report won't tell you who may have committed the homicide. I will say that there are times I am surprised once the police complete their work."

"I'm not sure I want to know that."

"I do need to get back. If you are available this coming weekend, I know that Sarah and I would love to have you for dinner. She will give you a call." Duffy gives me a cheek kiss before walking out the door. I sit for a few more minutes. Will Elsie be strong enough to read the autopsy report? Time to call Diana.

Chapter Fourteen

Next up, I hope to find a way to establish those connections at the Senior Services Care facility where John had spent the last six months of his life. I've considered a number of different strategies for why I am there talking to staff and residents. Visiting an old friend would be perfect, but I don't know anyone there. I'm too old to be applying for a job unless it would be as a volunteer. I'm sure even that would require going through a period of training, and we really don't have time for that. I hope my sister Eunice will forgive me for resurrecting her to shop for a care home for her. I'll make a point of putting extra flowers on her grave.

Many older women lose their sense of smell. That is why so many bathe themselves in perfume. I remember the Evening in Paris™ that my mother used when she reached that point in her life. I, however, have not lost that sense. I am hit with the hospital smell of alcohol and disinfectant the minute I open the door at Senior Services. I had called ahead to make an appointment with the administrator, Crystal Stratton for 9 AM. I wanted to arrive between meals, and after the staff had gotten their day started.

There are offices on either side of the front door as soon as I enter. The one to the left is labeled Administrator, but is closed. On the right side the door is marked Business Office. It has a large window where I can see two women at desks. Rather than knocking on the closed door, I decide to start at the business office. It will give me a chance to introduce myself, because I know I will want to chat with these women as much as I can. I affix a serious expression on my face as I open that door. One of the women looks up, smiles, and asks, "Can I help you?"

"I have a 9 AM appointment with Crystal Stratton."

"Oh, she just went down the hall to check on one of our residents. I'm sure she will be back shortly, but let me buzz her so that she knows you are here. You are welcome to take a seat while you wait."

I would love to jump in with a dozen questions, but I don't want to put these women on the defensive. I decide on basic chit chat. "It is a beautiful morning out there. I have the advantage of being able to go outside whenever I wish. At least you can see outside from your desks. That must make working in an office a little bit easier."

"You are right about that. If I were inputting numbers in a dark closed room, I would go nuts in an hour." This is said with a little giggle. "I consider this the best place to crunch those numbers."

"Does someone replace you at night? They would be running calculations in the dark."

The giggle is repeated, "Oh no. The business office closes at five and even Crystal leaves by six most nights."

The chit chat ends when the door to the business office opens as an attractive woman enters. "Mrs. Schmidel? I'm sorry to have kept you waiting." She extends a slim hand with hoop bracelets jingling on her wrist. "I'm Crystal Stratton. Why don't you come into my office where we can talk?" I feel almost like a giant as I follow her slim form out the door. She moves within an athletic grace that makes it hard to guess her age. Even her short, salt-and-pepper hair moves with energy. As I settle into the chair on the opposite side of her desk, I am struck by the kind look in her eyes. I feel guilty about lying as I start to tell her about needing care for my dear sister Eunice. I'm not sure if Eunice ever had a moment of memory loss before her death, but now I am spinning tales about the severity of her condition. I try not to tell too many lies, because I know they'll be hard to remember later. After a few minutes Crystal says, "Why don't we take a walk through the facility, so you can see what we have to offer? We can start with the physical therapy room and then the memory wing." As we make the tour, I am struck by how many of the residents seem pleased when Crystal stops to greet them or to pat them on the shoulder.

My feelings of guilt expand the minute Crystal keys in the code so we can enter the memory wing. Crystal bends over to greet a tiny little woman sitting in a wheelchair. The woman cocks her head as she looks up at me. A big smile spreads across her face and her big blue eyes sparkle as she says, "Myrtle, I haven't seen you in years. I remember how much fun we had at those dances when we were girls. I do hope you'll come back soon so we can talk. No one here remembers the old days like I do."

"Penny, Mrs. Schmidel and I are going to continue our tour. I'll be back to check on you later." Crystal pats Penny's hand before we walk away. As we continue down the hall, she says, "I'm sorry. Penny has some good days and some not so good ones. She likes to wait beside the door to greet all of us as we enter."

This might be the opportunity I've been looking for. "Penny might actually be having a very good day. I shared an apartment with my friend, Myrtle when we were girls. One of Myrtle's friends was named Penny. I don't know if this is that same woman, but I know Myrtle will want to come back to check."

"I'll hope that she is Penny's friend. I know Penny would enjoy having visitors. She no longer has any family. She does get lonely." Now I'll need Myrtle to be my partner in crime. No matter who Penny might be, she needs to be Myrtle's friend. We need to be able to visit the memory wing to see who could have gotten in to murder John. Just saying that word, gives me the willies.

Chapter Fifteen

"Have I got news to share!" Hattie barrels through my apartment door like a big truck ready to flatten any bump in its way. For a woman of only five foot four, she has a long, powerful stride, probably from the exercise she gets regularly. At seventy-four she is a full decade younger than many of our residents. One of her hobbies includes hiking with a Seattle area group. Today, however, I doubt if her news has anything to do with the hiking club. "Sorry that I'm late; to be honest I have one hell of a hangover." Her voice has the husky tone of a chronic smoker. "Mabel, I really need coffee if you have it. Tea isn't going to get the job done this morning." She takes a chair at the table with the rest of our team.

Florence reaches out to pat Hattie's hand, "I assume it was a rough night?"

"You're right about that. I started drinking at O'Brien's bar with the staff from John's old office at 4:30 in the afternoon. Later I joined the nurses who work at the home John was in. I probably shouldn't have joined both groups on the same day. I learned a lot from the office staff, but things the nurses shared are little fuzzy."

Betty picks up the orange marker as she pulls the whiteboard closer to herself. "We have started making notes about the things we've learned so far. I'm ready to add yours to the board." I try not to laugh when I think about Hattie's hair now being about that same shade of orange. I wonder if it is a planned color or just the result of taking out one color and putting in another. I remember my high school friends having either green or orange hair after changing too much.

"Well, the staff said John had gotten careless with the firm's money long before he retired. He decided to do pro bono work for the Xavier Onward Christian Ministry. He defended them in court about claims that they had defrauded members. This caused an uproar in the office with his partner Mark." Hattie looks quite proud of herself.

Having met Mark I have to ask, "The staff doesn't really think Mark would have murdered John now, do they?"

"No, but when Mark forced John to retire, there was money missing from the firm's accounts. The staff wondered if Mark hoped to get some of that money back from his estate. They didn't think Mark would murder John, but the missing money was still something that left bad feelings."

I didn't want to add what Elsie had told me about John's estate. She had said Mark knew there was no money left.

Betty squints at Hattie, "Okay, tell us what you learned from the nurses." She clearly has her look of 'teacher command' directed at Hattie.

Rather than look at Betty, Hattie studies the light that hangs over my table. I'm happy that I remembered to dust off the cobwebs that seem to pop up much too easily. "I told you that things there are bit fuzzy. They did mention an internal investigation into security measures. I have no idea what that involves or even if it is related."

"That can be something Myrtle and I check on when we returned to Senior Services later this week. We will be visiting a memory wing resident who might be an old friend of Myrtle's. She can be our cover for spending time there. Because I was originally asking about moving my sister there, I may not be in a good position to question the nursing staff. I'll see how that goes, but Hattie, you may have better luck with them."

"I can report that Elsie has scheduled John's graveside services for tomorrow morning. She said that the police finally released his body for the cremation," Betty announces in her teacher voice. "I'm hoping that most of us can attend. I'm sure that like in the crime shows, the police will be there. They need to know we support Elsie."

The discussion quickly turned to what each of my friends plans to wear, how we will all get to the cemetery, and the highlights of the best funerals we have ever attended. At this age, we have all attended far too many funerals.

Seattle is known for its drizzly rain, and today is no exception. If funerals weren't depressing enough, gray skies and drizzle adds a whole other level. Florence and I share a cup of coffee as we discussed strategy for packing five older women with wet umbrellas into each of our cars. Mr. Johnson will be transporting more of the women along with Elsie. I'm not sure that it is a good idea for Elsie to be seen riding with him. Diana had said the police already know that Elsie and Mr. Johnson have a relationship. They must have learned that fact when they first questioned Elsie and Mr. Johnson. It still angers me that John's son Brett refused to allow Elsie to ride in the funeral home limousine with him, his wife and his sister and brother-in-law. I can only hope that for Elsie's sake Brett behaves himself during the service. I'm sure the police will be watching from the sidelines.

Happily, the drizzle stops just before I pull into the cemetery drive. I am able to park three cars behind the hearse. I had advised my friends to wear comfortable shoes and not heels due to the soft ground. As I step out into a puddle, I realize I should've suggested we all wear boots. My friends all exit the car without incident. Myrtle decides to keep her umbrella closed, and use it as a cane. I hear Florence say, "Oh that wet grass has my shoes soaked instantly."

Betty exclaims, "Not only are my shoes wet, but now my feet are cold. Damn, I hate funerals. This is one of those days that I'm extra happy that I never married. Going to funerals for my own family and friends without adding those for a husband has been more than enough."

I turn to watch John's former partner, Mark, open Elsie's car door and take her hand to help her out of Mr. Johnson's car. He tucks her hand into his arm as they start to walk toward the grave. Once his passengers are all out of his car, Mr. Johnson scurries to join Mark and Elsie. He also offers her his arm. I see Brett staring daggers at her. Once the trio reaches the graveside both of the men step back to stand behind her. I hear Brett say, "Keep away from me. You have no right to be here after murdering my father!" Mark reaches out a hand to block Mr. Johnson who has his hands clutched into fists. I wonder what the police think of this display. Ethel must have thought the same thing. She walks over to chat with Clem's son, Dean who is Stan Mason's new partner. I can only hope she says the right things.

The service is a very short one, and we get back into the cars. Elsie had decided to host the reception in our banquet room. We have all pitched in to create the refreshments to help with her budget. I'm sure Brett didn't offer a penny toward the cost. Elsie had said that he even refused to pay any part of the funeral costs. She paid for him to ride in that limousine. Shameful.

Chapter Sixteen

Funerals are always sad; that is just a given. The receptions that follow, are usually quite varied and extremely interesting. Some are quiet with whispered condolences. Others are filled with heartfelt stories about adventures with the departed. The Irish are known for toasts with whiskey filled glasses raised in salute. As a child I had watched from afar the funeral and celebrations that followed the death of a Gypsy King. The caravans had filled the surrounding streets during the entire week. The city fathers were appalled, but we kids were fascinated. There was music, dancing, and even bonfires in the street. It left a striking memory. I would love to have my friends throw such an enthusiastic party after my death.

The reception today is a mixture. Brett had announced at the grave side service that neither he nor his sister would attend any gathering that included Elsie. I really don't think we will miss him. The residents of the St. James whisper quiet condolences to Elsie. None of us knew John, so we didn't have anything to say about him. Mark offers a few stories along with his raised glass. A couple of the other attorneys in attendance also offer short stories. Those stories were all about John in the early years of his career. They spoke of the respect they had for him. No one offers stories about the latter years. The men chat among themselves in a small group off to one side of the room. Because Myrtle is almost as tall as I am, I can easily find her despite the number of other women around us. I move to stand beside her so I can whisper in her ear, "Maybe you and I should strike up a conversation with at least one of these attorneys to aid in our investigation." She nods her head in agreement. Before we can take a step, I see Diana heading in their direction. Her height means that she is also easy to spot above the sea of short, white-haired women dressed in black. I am relieved that Diana is mingling with all of the attorneys. I do hope she gleans something that can be of value to us. Mark, cocks his head as she chats with him. I'm surprised when he turns toward me with a smile and a nod of his head. Myrtle raises an eyebrow in my direction. I can only shrug my shoulders. I have no idea what that smile means.

Looking around the room I decide that maybe we will make good detectives after all, because most people believe all old ladies look alike. I personally think that we offer some diversity as well as a range of sizes even if a select few of us are tall. White hair isn't even a given, since our younger members may still try to keep the gray away, and a couple of the much older are fond of blue, pink or purple. Betty's hair is still a light blue, but Hattie has switched to shades of purple. I'm happy to keep my hair white and cut short.

I join a group of my friends as they continue their discussion on the best and the worst funerals they had ever attended. Conflicts with relatives seemed to have been the main reason a funeral would be listed as the worst. I'm afraid this one will join that list. I still don't know how Brett can be so nasty to Elsie. She spent years of her life caring for John. Brett and his sister both have to know that. I am surprised that Elsie and John didn't have friends other than the attorneys who are in attendance. Did John keep Elsie so isolated that they did not have friends either as a couple or individually? That will be another question we may need ask.

The room slowly empties. Mark stops to shake my hand as he says goodbye. Myrtle gives me another raised eyebrow. Once only the residents remain, everyone pitches in, and the cleanup is done in short order. Betty announces that she needs a nap before she comes up to my apartment later for a cup of tea and another cookie. The investigative circle all nod their heads. I need to organize my thoughts before it is my turn to share. Have any of us learned anything in the last few days that may help Elsie? And what is Mark trying to tell me?

I have never considered myself a shrinking violet who would be unable to get in a word edgewise. That changes the minute I open my door to the members of our investigative team who are all trying to talk at once. As she storms in, Betty goes directly to the whiteboard to write down the things everyone is sharing. In just a few minutes she holds up her hand and uses that teacher voice, "Stop! Just stop! I can't understand you when you're all shouting at once. Now in alphabetical order quietly tell me what you learned."

I start laughing at the comical looks on the faces as each woman looks at another trying to arrange themselves in alphabetical order. Myrtle responds with, "If we are talking last names, then with Bailey, I would be first or still first with reverse alphabetical on first names. Either way I'm going first." By now all the women are laughing. It feels so good to lighten the mood after the sadness of the last few days.

Betty switches to the yellow marker as she looks at Myrtle expectantly. "I'm ready when you are."

"As you know Mabel and I went to the nursing home to visit a woman named Penny in the memory ward. I can't say that she was having a good day, nor can I say that she is the Penny I knew as a girl. She didn't recognize me, and I didn't recognize her. I hadn't really expected to after almost 70 years. To make matters worse she thought I was Elsie. She became quite agitated when she tried to tell me something that just came out in a jumble of words. The nurses asked us to come back another day. Poor Penny was extremely upset. I understand why they have locked doors for that ward."

I have to add, "There are days when I forget what I wanted when I walk into my kitchen, but I am so thankful that none of us are at the same point as poor Penny. With luck we will never be there. Myrtle and I do plan to go back soon. I want to have a better understanding of how someone might gain access to that wing of the home. I am also confident that Penny has something of value to share with us. It's too early to tell, but she could have actually seen John's killer."

"That fits with what I know," Ethel says, "I was going to tell you that the police have decided they need to question each of the residents in that wing. Dean told his father how difficult that was proving to be. They are focused on how John was smothered. They assume that one of the regular pillows had been used, but they haven't found the one."

"When I shared a drink with the nursing staff last night, they were still grumbling about the internal investigation into access to the memory wing," Hattie said. "The Care Center wants to make certain they don't have any liability into what happened. They are also doing a review of deaths that have occurred over the last few years. The staff assumes they are looking for a pattern which would imply an 'angel of death' at the center."

It was finally Florence's turn. "Elsie gave me five years' worth of their bank statements. It will take me a while to organize the information. At first glance there was a fair amount of cash in the accounts five years ago, but it dropped sharply until the deposit from the sale of the house. I will want to separate regular household expenses from the big withdrawals that I know are there. That's all I can say for now."

I decide it is time to address the elephant in the room. "Do we think it is even possible for Elsie to have physically done this to John? I know that I am tall enough to lean over and reach him in a hospital bed, but could Elsie do that?"

Florence is the first to respond, "I'm the same size as Elsie. I could not have done that unless I had climbed up on the bed. Even then I'm not sure I'd have the strength if he fought back at all."

Ethel said, "I agree. I wanted to give my husband a kiss after he died, but I would have needed to stand on a chair to reach him. Hospital beds were never designed for short women to help their loved ones. I don't see how the police can possibly think she did this."

The mood around my table has become very solemn. Each of us are reminded of the struggles an older woman can have in trying to manage both her money and the details of her life. It is time for us to focus on what's next. "I don't think we have anything to report to Diana yet. Hopefully we will have more information in a couple more days. Can I offer anyone more tea or cookies?"

Chapter Seventeen

Penny is again waiting just inside the double doors of the memory unit. I feel hopeful as she reaches out to take Myrtle's hand. "Oh, Myrtle I'm so glad you came. Let's go to my room because I have something important to tell you." We have gone no more than ten paces down the hall before Penny stops her wheelchair and turns to look at Myrtle. She has a confused look on her face as she then looks at me. "Myrtle and I need to hurry so we are not late for Mr. Williams' Social Studies class. You aren't in our class. Where do you belong?"

My hopeful feeling flits away like a butterfly. I pat Penny on the shoulder. She seems so very fragile. "I'm just visiting today. I thought I would join you and Myrtle. Shall we go?"

Halfway down the hall Penny stops again, and opens a door into what I assume is her room. She rolls in ahead of us and then turns. "This is my room, and we aren't in high school anymore. I remember reading that Mr. Williams just died. That must be why he was on my mind. He was a very good teacher. I read that he was over 100 years old when he died. I wonder if John Hansen knew Mr. Williams. John just died as well." She looks so sad, before she continues. "There was something about John I wanted to tell you, but all I can think about is Mr. Williams. It may be another day before I remember what it was about John."

If Elsie had to watch John go through something like this, it is no wonder she wanted to escape to the St. James. Such swings of memory and emotions are so hard to watch on a woman I didn't know in younger days. This makes me want to help Elsie even more than before.

We chat with Penny for a few more minutes. She knows where she is, and who she thinks we are, but can't remember what she wanted to tell Myrtle. She is starting to look tired. Before I can even suggest that we leave, her head droops. She has fallen asleep. We meet the nurse outside in the hallway. I watch as she uses the keypad to unlock the door so we can leave. I wonder how often the Center changes that code. That information may be important in our investigation.

Betty is fifteen minutes early for our get-together. She has a very determined look on her face as she marches into my apartment. "Everyone needs to get here fast. I have important information I need to share. We need to pick up the pace on our investigation."

Before I can even close the door, Florence comes in with a delighted smile on her face. "I've been looking at the numbers, and I also have something to share. Mabel, can you send everyone a text moving up our start time? This is important."

Before I even finished typing, Florence goes to the door as the rest of our team comes piling in all talking at once. This will clearly be a productive meeting. Betty jumps to her feet and shouts, "I go first, because my information is the most important! Mr. Johnson was still in Elsie's apartment when the police arrived this morning to talk to her. Detective Mason stayed in her apartment while his partner took Mr. Johnson to his. I didn't see Diana join her which worries me. Both detectives were there for almost 45 minutes. Once they left, Mr. Johnson returned to Elsie's apartment. I didn't knock to disturb them."

"I'm next," says Florence. "I'm not a forensic accountant, but I'm beginning to think the police should use one on these accounts. I found some irregularities that disturb me going back a good five years. There were large withdrawals where the signature doesn't appear to be John Hansen's signature. Hopefully these are not checks that Elsie signed in his name. Some of them were written to his son. I'm sure Elsie would have told me about money given to Brett. Others were written to a collection of people and companies including that Ministry you mentioned. I haven't established a pattern, but together it is a lot of money."

Hattie rises to her feet as the women again all try to talk at once. She raps her knuckles against the table to get everyone's attention. "That might fit with what I learned from the people in John's practice last night. The police are still questioning all of them about John's time at the office. None of them seemed to like Brett. One secretary said he was slimy. They often heard loud voices when he would visit his father. They claimed they didn't know what the arguments were about, but that the voices were clearly arguing."

It is Myrtle's turn. She doesn't display the same excitement that the other women had; her voice is soft and sad, "We haven't learned anything that important yet. Penny, my old friend, who lives in the Care Center, tried to remember something she wanted to tell us about John. Unfortunately, the only thing she remembered when we visited was there was something she knew was important."

I add, "I think we need to find a way to have the police look at those bank records after Florence finishes what she can. I'm not sure if they will consider other aspects of the financial angle unless we have something concrete. I also seriously doubt if they will take the time to question Penny about what she knows. If she is having a bad day when they question her, they will assume she has nothing to tell them. I should probably call Diana to make certain that Elsie lets her know about that police visit. We have a lot more work to do." Despite everything we have learned, we don't have a serious list of suspects. I worry that Elsie and Mr. Johnson are still at the top of the suspect list for the police.

Chapter Eighteen

It is time for another poker party. As I check the cupboard for supplies, I realize I need to do one of two things. I need to buy more candy or become a better poker player. Thank goodness we don't play for money! I also realize that I am stalling. I really should call Diana to see if Elsie told her about the most recent police visit. I can kill two birds with one stone by inviting her to the poker party. That way she won't think I'm just calling to tattle on Elsie. That is what I'm doing, but I really don't want the reputation of being a tattletale.

The call to Diana, unfortunately, goes the way I had expected it to. Will we ever be able to convince Elsie that she is in peril? Diana quickly went from jovial laughing at the invitation to play poker to her controlled legal voice. I don't think I would want to be listening in on the lecture I'm sure Diana will give Elsie. I've never gotten the impression that Elsie lacks intelligence, but as time goes on, I suspect there has been more emotional abuse than she originally shared. It is time I asked her for details about her first marriage. I believe that the only way we will be able to help her is if we truly know her history. I think I need to invite her up for tea to have that discussion. I can ask her to help me plan the poker party.

About forty-five minutes later I am startled when my phone dings with an incoming text. I have been mixing a batch of my peanut butter oatmeal recovery cookies on auto pilot. I do hope I have remembered to add all of the correct ingredients. This is a clear reminder of how concerned I am about Elsie. Operating on autopilot can be dangerous especially for a mature woman. Mature, hell, it is time I acknowledge that I am an old woman. At least I am not trying to pretend that I am middle aged. No one lives to be 170. I loved that line from "On Golden Pond."

As I suspected, the text is from Diana. She says, 'Thank you. I think I have Elsie back on track. She has also finally agreed to request a copy of the autopsy report. It may not tell us anything we don't know, but having it will put us on the same plane with the police. Will she be at the poker party?'

I reply, 'I had planned to invite her unless you think that is a bad idea.'

Diana replies, 'I think it might be a very good idea if everyone is reminding her to call me. I don't know why she resists doing that.'

I end the discussion with, 'I'll talk with her today. I will let you know if I learn anything important.'

When I open the door, I think maybe Diana has had an effect on Elsie. Her eyes are downcast at the floor rather than at me in what I assume is either a guilty or ashamed look. "Elsie dear, I'm so glad you could join me for tea. Come in, please." She glances at me out of the corner of her eye as she walks into my living room. She is clearly nervous as she twists a handkerchief in her hands. "Let's sit at the table by the window while we have our tea. I think it will be cozier while we talk." Do I share that I have talked to Diana? Elsie still has not actually looked at me. It may be harder to ask my questions than I had thought.

I sit the tea and the plate of cookies on the table. I take it as an encouraging sign as Elsie mumbles, "Thank you." She wraps her hands around the teacup as if it were a lifeline for a drowning woman.

I decide to jump in with blunt questions. I can see no other way if we are going to help her. "You do know that we all want to help you, don't you Elsie?"

Elsie continues to look at her hands wrapped around her teacup before answering in a very quiet voice, "I know that, Mabel, but I'm not sure anyone can actually help me. The police truly believe that I murdered John."

"Why don't you tell me about your first marriage? You really have never shared much about any parts of your life. Why don't I start by telling you how I met my George? Myrtle and I were sharing an apartment in a small town in Eastern Washington. We both had jobs where we hoped we would meet our future husbands. So many of the boys who had graduated with us had been drafted to serve in the Korean War. Neither of us thought that any of those boys had much to offer as husbands. We decided to accept an invitation to a USO dance at the Ordinance Depot. The Depot employed a lot of civilians from area towns, but there were also many soldiers there as well. We remembered hearing older girls talk about meeting the soldiers at the World War II USO dances when we were still in grade school. I'm afraid we had an idealistic view of what those dances would be like.

"The Depot was seven miles outside of town, and the USO sent a bus to pick up the fifteen of us girls for the dance on a rainy Saturday night. I'm sure our fathers would not have been happy if they had known we were on that bus. We were all giggly with excitement as the bus proceeded along the twisty highway that led to the Depot. Access to the depot itself was by a narrow gravel road that was built during World War I, maintained through World War II, but had not been maintained since the start of the Korean war. The road had many potholes and standing water in the ditches along the sides. A deer darted across the road, and the bus driver swerved to avoid it sending the bus into one of those ditches. The water and mud covered the door to the bus. We were all scrambling to get out of the seats on the ditch side as that water seeped in. The driver climbed out one of the emergency windows to walk to the gate to request help.

"It seemed like forever before a group of soldiers arrived to rescue us. One soldier was inside the bus who helped us climb out that same emergency window into the arms of a waiting soldier. That is how I met my George. He carried me to the truck that took us the rest of the way to the dance. Not a single one of the girls had a spot of mud on their shoes, but those poor soldiers had mud to their knees. George later told me that it was good preparation for what awaited them in Korea. While we danced, he also told me that I was the most beautiful girl he'd ever met. Three months later he left for Korea. We exchanged letters all of the time he was there. I think those letters helped us to truly know each other before we married after the war. When first the 'MASH' movie and later the television show came out, I wanted to believe that George was as heroic as those doctors, but had remained faithful to me. During all of the years of our marriage, I never had reason to doubt him. Why don't you tell me how you met your first husband? What was his name again?"

Chapter Nineteen

"Meeting my first husband, Harold, was nowhere near as romantic as your story. I was twenty-five with a job in the fabric department of JCPenney's. I still lived at home, and my mother had started to refer to me as an old maid. My aunt used to tell me I was too homely for any man to want me. She is the one who introduced us. He was the real estate agent who sold my grandmother's house after she passed. He was in his late-30s, and I thought he was so sophisticated as well as handsome. Now I would see it all as a slick con-man's façade. My father said that he did not like Harold. My mother, however, said that if Harold asked me to marry him, I needed to say yes because I would not get a better offer. During the months that we dated, he took me to fancy dinners, plays, and even Broadway shows that were touring in Seattle. We were often joined by some of his male friends and their dates. I remember that I noted that none of the men were married even though some of them were older than Harold. I thought it was strange, but I did not consider it significant until after we were married.

"The wedding was a large fancy church wedding six months after we started dating. I truly thought I was the luckiest girl in the world. He was tall with very broad shoulders, and I felt like a little kitten tucked under his arm. He made a big production about having our wedding announcement in all of the papers as well as information about our whirl-wind tour of Europe for our honeymoon. I went from feeling lucky to being mystified and ashamed at the status of our marriage even though it took me two full years to truly understand what was happening. I had been a twenty-five-year-old virgin, and honestly didn't know what to expect of marital relations. We had sex on our wedding night. I can't say that he made love to me. I quickly realized there was no love involved. When he finished, he got up and said that the marriage had now been consummated. It was only later that I realized that meant I could not have the marriage annulled, and that I would be too embarrassed to ever divorce him. Every night of our so-called honeymoon, he left me to spend half the night in one of the local bars. I assumed he was with prostitutes that he met there. It was only after we returned home, and he repeated that pattern, but was leaving each night with one of those male friends, that I realized the truth. I kept thinking there was something wrong with me, only to conclude that my true fault was being female.

"When I threatened to leave him, he started to treat me a little better. He begged me not to tell either set of our parents about the men in his life. He only went out one or two nights per week, and wanted to cuddle in bed with me on the other nights. As long as he didn't smell like some foreign, cheap aftershave, I was willing to settle for so little. I gave up my job to become a housewife even though we were never to have children. I didn't even have girlfriends. He was terrified that I might tell a friend about his secret. I kept that secret for almost 30 years, until he came home one night to tell me that he had fallen in love and wanted his lover to move in with us. I told him I couldn't do that. I didn't know how I could pretend under those circumstances. Little did I know that it would get much worse. He and his lover had an argument when Harold told him that I couldn't agree to the three of us living together. His lover choked him to death. The story made the news for months. I was so mortified; I couldn't force myself to leave the house. Going to the trial was out of the question; I didn't want to know any of the details. I couldn't even read the newspapers. I had kept his secret for decades to have it come out as such sordid fodder. How could he do that to me? I only learned the truth about the argument months after his lover was convicted. The man actually sent me a letter to tell me how sorry he was. At least in Harold's will he had left me that house and enough assets that I didn't have to worry about a job for a long time. Part of me is still so angry at myself for throwing away my life for all of those years. And yet, I did almost the same thing when I met John."

By now, I am working very hard to close my mouth. I was not prepared for this story about Elsie's first marriage. She didn't even give me a chance to insert a comment during her narrative. I'm not sure what I would've said if she'd given me that chance. I'll leave it to Diana to worry about how this might impact the investigation into John's death. I'm almost afraid to ask her more questions about how she met and married John. I don't have to wait long before she volunteers that information.

Chapter Twenty

"Over the next ten years I worked as a sales clerk in a local department store. I spent time in my garden, went to church every week but didn't volunteer with any of the church activities. I visited my parents every Sunday afternoon as was expected. My mother kept suggesting that I sell the house, and move away where no one would know about my embarrassing history with Harold. I may not have had any friends, but I really didn't want to start over again somewhere else. I did sell the house, but bought a condo in exchange. My mother claimed that she had been the one who didn't like Harold rather than my father. He never had anything to say about the matter right up to and including the day he died.

"I honestly didn't think there was any reason I needed to attend the reading of my father's will. I was confident that he would leave everything to my mother, but she asked me to be there with her. John was my father's attorney. I was surprised when John read the details. Although he left the majority of his estate to my mother, my father had left me the stocks and bonds that were in his safety deposit box. My mother seemed surprised that there was a deposit box in my father's name only. John stated that he would be happy to accompany me to the bank with a copy of the will so that I could access that box. He gave me a big smile when he made that statement. I couldn't determine if my mother was pleased about his attention or angry about the whole situation.

"John was very courteous during that bank visit. He offered to take those stocks and bonds back to the office with him to determine their value. I was happy to let him do so because I had no idea where to even begin. Two weeks later he called me back to his office where he presented me with a check for $3,000. He said he had liquidated those stocks and bonds and the check represented the proceeds minus the fee for his services. He did not provide me with an accounting of the transaction. I didn't question him. I put my trust in him because he was my father's attorney. Six months later we repeated this same pattern when my mother passed. My parents had been older when I was born. I had no siblings and so everything was left to me once probate had been settled. John again stepped up to handle all of the details. Again, he liquidated things and told me that this time he would invest the money for me. It should have been a red flag, but he had already asked me to marry him. I trusted him. We married just after my mother's estate was settled. I didn't know that he had put that money into his own accounts. Even if I had known, there was nothing I could do as his wife. What was mine became his, and what was his, continued to be his. I didn't learn the true extent of this until just before I moved here. John and I were married for almost 15 years.

"I had married him because I found him to be warm, affectionate, and considerate. I married looking for the romance that I had been denied in all of the years I was married to Harold. Unlike Harold, John had no problem in making sure we had marital relations. His affection and consideration ended as soon as the judge had declared us man and wife. I had heard the expression 'slam, bam, and thank you ma'am,' but had no idea what it really meant until our wedding night. As soon as he was done, he rolled over on his side away from me and dozed off. I cried myself to sleep. I actually missed the nights of cuddling in bed with Harold. In the days and years that followed, I knew that John expected sex when he would be laying on his back as I slipped into bed. I was expected to do my duty as his wife, and not to ask for anything more from him.

"He must've known I was neither happy nor satisfied with the terms of our marriage. Like Harold, he expected me to quit my job and stay home to take care of his needs and his house. He quickly sold my condo, and transferred the proceeds and all of my other assets into his bank accounts. He gave me an allowance to use for grocery shopping and any of my personal needs. He took care of all of our financial arrangements. Although I was home and received the mail, I was not to open anything that was addressed to him such as the bank statements, utility bills or tax statements. When he filed our income tax forms, he told me they were too complicated for me to comprehend. His quote was 'Don't worry your pretty little head about things you don't understand.' I was to sign without reading those tax forms. By this time, we had been married for about two years. That was when I learned that my car was no longer mine. I had been stopped by a police officer for going thirty-five in a 30-mile zone. The officer asked for my registration and insurance card. The registration showed the car to be only in John's name, but my name was on the insurance card along with his. I tried to check some of our other major assets, but it wasn't easy. It took me years to learn that nothing was in my name. I was trapped. I had no job and no money. I couldn't even save out a little money from my weekly grocery allowance. John made me give him the receipts for every penny that I spent. He said he checked them to make certain I was making good decisions. When I spent twenty dollars to buy a dress, he made me return it because he didn't feel I needed it. I had lost thirty pounds, and my clothes just hung on me. His response was to buy a used sewing machine, and told me to start taking in the dresses that I had. I had not used a sewing machine since my home economics class in junior high school. I didn't even know how to make those types of alterations, but I learned. I had no other choice. I was able to convince him to let me buy some things at thrift shops as long as I did not spend more than ten dollars a month on my clothes there."

My first thoughts are concerns about how the police would use the story as the motive for Elsie to have killed John. My second thought is that she could not have physically smothered him. She might have when she first married John, but after that 30-pound loss I suspect that she weighs about 90 pounds. I reach out to take both of her hands in mine as I pull her to her feet. I bend down to give her a hug. “Oh Elsie, I have heard of controlling men, but this is just too much. I think I need something stronger than tea, if you have more of your story to tell.”

“There is more. Do you have any brandy?”

Chapter Twenty-One

A shot of peach brandy should give our tea the boost we need for Elsie to continue her story. "I'm ready to listen if you're ready to share more."

"These are things I have never told anyone. We had been married about four years when I noticed that John seemed to be forgetting things. He would forget that we were going to a function with some of his friends until one of them would call to ask when we would arrive. He would invite his daughter and her husband or his son and daughter-in-law for dinner without telling me. Brett would make snide comments when I would throw together a fast spaghetti dinner or simple casserole. At least John would have gotten the time right for the invitation, so that we had not already eaten dinner ourselves. He expected me to find his keys. He had started to leave them in odd places. One day I found them in the cookie jar, and on another in one of the planters beside the front door. He made an extra copy of his office keys, so that he could still go to work in either car with my keys.

"Added to all of that, he seemed to be angry most of the time. I tried even harder to meet his expectations, but it didn't seem to be enough. He never hit me. He would, however, ball his hand into a fist and shake it in my face. He was so much bigger and stronger than I was, that I was truly afraid that he was going to hurt me. He would tell Brett what a terrible wife I was, and how useless I was. Brett seemed to take pleasure in re-telling me what John had said, but only when John was not in the room. Brett started to drop by more often without his wife. He and John would go to John's home office. If John was the last one to enter the room, he would not always remember to close the door. I'll confess that I started to eavesdrop whenever possible. Brett would say that something had come up and he needed a loan against his future inheritance. John would faithfully write a check. I had no way of knowing how much money John was giving to Brett, but I was concerned."

"I would have been concerned as well. George and I thought we had saved more than enough for a comfortable retirement. Now I realize that what we had saved could never have covered all of our plans in today's dollars. We did get to make that transatlantic cruise, but never did the grand tour of Europe that had been at the top of our list. Now I still have enough money to live comfortably as long as I don't take extravagant trips."

"I would have been delighted if we had those types of plans. Seven years after I first noticed John's memory issues, his partners demanded that he see a doctor. The doctor confirmed what I already knew; John had Alzheimer's. He had progressed from mild to middle stage. Over the previous two years, he had relied on me to drive him to work. He was often confused about where he was and where he was going. John tried to deny the diagnosis, but his partners called me, and I told them the truth. They demanded that he retire. I became even more concerned about our finances, but John was not ready to let me access that information. With John home 24/7, it became even harder for me to determine just where we stood financially. It took another two years before I had a chance to occasionally check the mail before John got to it. That is when I started to guess about how much money he was still giving to Brett, and how much he was giving to that Xavier Onward Christian Ministry referenced in his will. I also saw checks to companies that I had never heard of. I couldn't even find them on the Internet. Those checks were smaller. The ones to Brett and the Ministry were my main concern."

I decided against sharing with Elsie that we had learned about the money John had misused while he was still at his practice. I'm sure he was one of the Xavier's favorite donors.

"I told John that I needed to go to the doctor because I wasn't feeling well. I didn't really feel comfortable at leaving him alone at home, but I needed documentation of his Alzheimer's from his doctor to take to my own lawyer. I would need a court order to have my name added to our bank accounts. That took another six months. At least by then John was no longer fighting me. That was also when I got the first shut off notice for utilities that John had stopped paying. I signed the checks to pay those bills, and luckily the bank didn't question them. Once I had the accounts in both of our names, I was able to see the thousands of dollars that he had given to Brett and to that Ministry. I had to tell Brett that we could no longer give him money. I did not realize that he had started to sign John's name on checks. Once I took the time to look closely at the accounts, I discovered there were blank checks missing."

I couldn't hold back, "It sounds like Brett had either a drug or gambling problem, but either way you should have had him arrested for the theft."

"I know you're right, but John was my husband and Brett is still my stepson. I just couldn't do that. Then John fell and broke his hip. I had no choice but to put him in the nursing home. That was when I knew I had to sell the house. It was only after the realtor ordered a title report, that I learned John had mortgaged the house for almost its full value. What little money was left went for John's care while I waited for Medicaid to kick in. I moved into the St. James with nothing."

Oh, dear me, this was worse than I thought. Now Elsie's comments at the reading of John's will make so much more sense. By this time Elsie looks exhausted. I pat her shoulder as I help her to her feet. I don't want her to fall, so I walk her back to her apartment. Once I have done that, I will call Diana. I'm not sure what her reaction will be when I fill in the details about Elsie's two marriages. I will also have to add Mark and possibly John's clients to our suspect list. If John had stolen money from the law firm, it may have been from clients. Like Elsie, they may not have known just what he had done until recently. Brett clearly needed to be on the list as well. I know we will need more facts before Stan Mason will even listen to our theories.

Chapter Twenty-Two

"Please, repeat that again slowly. What did Elsie say about the death of her first husband? That is not a topic we've discussed." Diana's normal level voice has more than a touch of anger. So far, the phone call is pretty much what I expected.

"In a nutshell, his gay lover choked him to death. It was ten years before Elsie met and married her second husband John. How do you think the police will react if they learn about this?"

"I've never known Stan Mason to overlook a back story that might very well be a reason for murder. The only thing that would make it worse was if John had been that gay lover. Stan would have learned about all of this when he ran Elsie's name through the system. I wonder why he hasn't said anything about it?"

"Is this something you think our investigative team needs to know about? You are the only person I have told. Most of our team members will be at the poker party tomorrow night. I wasn't planning to have discussions about our investigation. I did want the team members to encourage Elsie to keep you close whenever the police talk to her. Do you still plan to come?"

"I clearly need help with convincing Elsie to call me before talking to the police, so I will be there to play poker. For now, keep Elsie's first marriage to yourself. I want to put in a call to Stan, but I'm not sure how much he will share with me."

"You might want to call Ethel, rather than Stan. She might have information through Clem and/or his son."

I love the sound of Diana's laugh. "That may very well be the best plan. I'll make that call right now, thank you."

Less than five minutes later Diana calls me back. "I don't know how Ethel does it, but she was a wealth of information. It seems Dean had told his dad about the messy end to Elsie's first husband. He added that Stan doesn't consider that first marriage a factor in John's death. It does appear that Elsie is still the prime suspect."

"I will tell the poker players to double their efforts in our investigation, but to not ask Elsie about her first marriage. They may have questions about John's dementia, but we'll cross that bridge when we come to it. I think I need a nap."

"Why don't you do that. I'm making chicken for dinner if you would like to join me. I'm just not in the mood for the hustle and bustle of eating out tonight. I think I could use the company especially the way you take things in stride. Will you come?"

"What time and what can I bring?"

"6:30, and some of your fabulous cookies if they are available."

"It's a date."

Terry Thompson had completed his work on the St. James and started to rent out the apartments almost 4 years ago. I still consider myself so lucky to have seen his first advertisement for a newly renovated two-bedroom apartment at what I consider a bargain rate. I only needed to look at the unit for a few minutes before I wrote a check for my deposit. As soon as I got back to my car, I had shared the information with my circle of friends. I still take delight in having so many of those women as my neighbors. Diana was not one of them. I'm not actually sure when she moved in, because I rarely saw her. Rumor had it that she had taken an extended trip to Europe just after moving into her apartment. This will be my chance to get to know the woman rather than just the lawyer.

I am wrapped in the rich aroma of rosemary, thyme, and garlic the minute Diana opens the door. Her normal jeans and T-shirt are topped with a long red and white striped apron. She waves me in with the wooden spoon in her hand. "I adore a woman who is punctual. Proves that you are definitely not a diva. I was remiss, however, in that I hadn't asked if you had any food dislikes or allergies."

I laugh as I step into her colorful living room. I note the collection of interesting objects displayed amongst the books in the floor to ceiling shelves, before I answer. "I'll eat almost anything especially if someone else is fixing it. I still cook for myself, but it tends to be rather basic dull entrées. Whatever you are cooking smells divine."

"Tonight, I felt like revisiting the memories of my trip to France. Dinner is Coq Au Vin. It is almost ready. Would you care for glass of chardonnay along with some cheese and crackers to start us off?"

"That sounds delightful. I'll confess I am jealous. My late husband and I had talked about going to Europe, but it wasn't something we ever did. How long ago was it that you were in France?"

"My last trip there was nine months ago. I was in Paris for a month of cooking classes. They were taught in the kitchen of a charming inn where I had stayed on my prior trip."

By now I have surveyed most of the colorful posters decorating the walls in every direction. "Have you also been to Greece and to Tuscany?"

"Yes, with more cooking classes thrown in for good measure. It has become my passion. Please, take a seat, make yourself comfortable." As I take a sip of the wine Diana hands me, I think I'm going to enjoy a very comfortable evening.

Chapter Twenty-Three

Dinner tastes even better than it smells. "My complements to the chef! This is wonderful. Do I really need to go to France to take a cooking class to make this the right way?"

Diana gives me a big smile as she laughs, "No. With the way you bake cookies, I'm sure you can follow a recipe and then experiment to make it your own. To be honest, the only reason I booked European cooking classes was to ensure that I would not be asked to cancel my vacation plans at the last minute. I learned that lesson the hard way my first three years with that partnership. I'd plan my trip, and then at the last minute I'd be assigned an important case that required all of my time instantly. That got old very quickly. My grandmother always told me to make her proud, but to make time for my own needs."

"Sounds like a very wise grandmother. I detect a hint of an accent that I haven't been able to place. Where did you grow up?"

"Kentucky. That is where I also first learned to cook. My grandmother had me on a stool beside her every Sunday when we fixed a big dinner for the extended family. My good Baptist grandmother had hundreds of recipes that called for a healthy shot of the best Kentucky bourbon she could buy. I also heard the Baptist preacher give rousing Sunday morning sermons on the evils of drink. I often wondered if those were directed at her. She had no problem going into the liquor store to buy her bourbon. I learned a lot about being a strong woman from her. Plus, she taught me how to keep the courage of my convictions no matter what. She has always been my inspiration."

This makes me laugh. "I moved from the west coast to the Midwest when my husband started med school in

Chicago. When it was time to set up his medical practice, he said that he had more opportunities in Seattle, so we returned. What brought you this direction?"

"Law school. The University of Washington in Seattle was more welcoming to female students than the more traditional schools in the early 1970's. Ruth Bader Ginsberg may have fought her way through east coast schools in the 1950's but I decided law school itself would be hard enough without adding that extra layer of discrimination as a black woman. Remember, it wasn't until I graduated, that a woman could sign for a student loan without a male cosigner. My father thought I was nuts to even try, but he signed all of those forms as my cosigner. We were both shocked when I was hired by a local firm as soon as I passed the bar. Of course, the men who graduated with me had offers before they even graduated. I don't miss those days."

"I had forgotten that because we were married, George had to give his consent for me to enroll in nurses training. He was so generous, I never paid attention to the limitations women had back then. That is not a topic I want to bring up at the poker party! Betty will be standing in the middle of the table yelling about how bad it was!"

Thank goodness Diana didn't have a mouth full of wine because her laugh would have sent it to the ceiling. "I don't really know Betty all that well, but well enough to picture that! That is just too funny. Young women today really don't understand what all of that meant back then, and may they never need to experience it."

I take a deep breath because it is time to address the secrets I've yet to share. "I told you about how her first marriage ended, but has Elsie told you about John's mismanagement of finances during their marriage?"

"No, but I figured we would end up here. What do I need to know that she hasn't told me?" I suggest cookies and tea as we settle in for a long conversation.

Two days later the poker party is in full swing, when there is loud knocking on my door. All of my invitees are seated around the table except for Ethel who said she had a special date planned with Clem. I have no idea who could be at my door. I instantly reject the idea that the police could be coming to arrest Elsie. I don't want a bad thought to produce a bad result. The knocking doesn't stop until the minute I open the door. Ethel races in waving her arms in the air. "Elsie! Elsie, Dan just told me they have taken you off their prime suspect list. They are finally convinced you could not physically have done that to John. They have, however, moved Mr. Johnson to the head of the list as a person with a strong motive. It is time for us to turn our attention to saving Mr. Johnson."

Chapter Twenty-Four

Saving Mr. Johnson sounds like such a simple task, because we are confident that we are great detectives, and that he did not kill John. This means, however, that I will have to face facts I really didn't want to know. Mr. Johnson seems to be a nice man, a decent apartment manager (even if he only wants to rent to women) and extremely discrete about his relationships in the building. If we are going to help him, we will have to lay out more information about him than I really ever wanted to know. Asking Elsie about both of her marriages was bad enough. We will clearly need to show that he has a pattern of girlfriends rather than a fixation on just Elsie. At least I hope he doesn't have a fixation on just her.

The poker party quickly turns in to a true party as everyone starts congratulating Elsie. I notice that Diana has not joined in the festive mood. Then the reality that Mr. Johnson could be in peril dims the party atmosphere for all of the ladies. Diana and Elsie quietly lead the others to the elevator. Florence stays long enough to help me clean up. As we stack the dirty dishes, she turns to me, "Mable, is this a case of one step forward and two back?"

"I honestly don't know, but I'm having similar thoughts. I think I'll have a serious chat with Diana in the morning. She may have a better take on this than we do."

Florence says over her shoulder as she opens my door to leave, "I hope she has something good to say."

"I'll let you know." I have a feeling that I won't sleep well tonight.

My morning walk is not as relaxing as it normally is. Even the twittering of the birds is not enough to chase concerns for Elsie from my mind. As I had done most of the night, I vacillate between thinking the police will just focus on Mr. Johnson and believing that if they focus on him, they will still consider Elsie his partner.

As I knock on Diana's door, I wish I had asked her to join me on my walk. Doing so, might have made it easier to ask my questions. When she opens the door, I try to remember to smile. That seems like more than a little bit of effort this morning. "Mable, I've been expecting you. Please come in. Can I offer you a cup of coffee?" I'm afraid that my voice has escaped me, so I just nod my head. "Come join me in the kitchen while I fill our cups."

I settle myself on one of the stools at the island. This is when I'm reminded that Terry had a design flaw for little old ladies. The counter bar is at that fashionable 42-inch height, which means the barstools are also high. I have no problem parking my butt there, but know that most of the women in the building would find it difficult. I take a deep breath and quit stalling. "Diana, I'm concerned that having the police shift their focus to Mr. Johnson does not really reduce the threat for Elsie. Do you think they will consider the two of them partners in crime?"

Diana places a mug of coffee on the bar in front of me. "If I remember correctly, you take your coffee black. Is that correct?"

Is it her turn to stall for a minute? "Black is correct, but after the sleepless night I had, I should give thought to a shot or two of Bailey's in the hopes of taking a long afternoon nap."

"About 2 AM, I thought about giving you a call. You could have joined me as I paced the floor worrying about both Elsie and Mr. Johnson. I honestly thought that when I quit practicing law full-time, I would be done with pacing the floor trying to find an angle to help my clients. After reading the autopsy report, if I were the District Attorney I would be looking seriously at Mr. Johnson. The report said there was considerable force used to smother John. We know Elsie could not have done that. I would, however, be considering both Elsie and Mr. Johnson in a conspiracy to commit the murder. I'm afraid it will take more than me to get both of them out of this mess. I don't see what either of them would have to gain from her husband's death. When do you call the next meeting of the investigation team? I think Ken Smith will need any information we can gather. I'll call him later to see how I can help."

"I'll go mix up a batch of recovery cookies before I call the team. Hopefully we can meet later this afternoon. Good luck with your call to Mr. Smith."

I send out the group text as I mix the cookie dough. I'm hoping that everyone can come at 3 PM. That should give me time to take that long nap with my apartment filled with the smell of freshly baked cookies.

Chapter Twenty-Five

Diana displays a sad expression rather than her normal lawyer-neutral look as she rises to her feet. The team members have looks of concern as they turn in her direction. "I have spoken with Mr. Johnson's attorney, Ken Smith. We both agree that not only is Mr. Johnson in peril, but that Elsie is not out of the woods yet. Our concern is that the police will think the two of them formed a conspiracy to commit the murder. Although I would normally never recommend amateurs to play at being detectives, I'm hopeful that the group of us can find reasons that the police should look in a different direction. Myrtle, you said that your old friend at the Care Center wanted to tell you something she felt was important. The police will never consider her a reliable witness, but her information may help us find someone who may be such a witness. Hattie, we also need to know if they have found a pattern of death at the center that might mean the guilty party could be a resident or staff member there. I believe you said the staff was looking into that possibility. Can you follow up with them? Ethel, can you check with Clem to see if his son has shared any more information about the direction the police are taking? Anyone have any other ideas of how we can push this investigation along?"

The moment has come. I really didn't ever want to say this, but I don't see any other way. "I think we need to create a pattern for Mr. Johnson's relationships. Do any of you actually know when he started dating each of our residents? Do you know how long each of those lasted, and how long it took before he started a new one? I will ask Elsie for exactly when she started dating him."

"I know exactly how long I dated him, and exactly when we broke up." Ethel has a big smile on her face. "I broke up with him the day I first met Clem. I knew that I really wanted a long-term relationship rather than just a little bit of fun. Zeb made me feel proud to be a mature woman, but I wanted so much more than he had to offer. I think each of the women he dated feels the same way. I have no problem asking for those details. My only concern is that he and Elsie have been together for what I think may be an exception to his pattern."

"Oh dear," Hattie says with a frown on her face. "I was hoping that I was the only one who had noticed that about Zeb and Elsie. The two months I spent with him were fun, but I decided that I really wanted to be free to date anyone I met. Betty, if you want to start a new list, I will provide you with the dates. Ethel, do you want to divide up the residents, so we don't miss anyone? It is possible we didn't know about everyone."

"That works for me. I'll take the first and second floors if you do the third and fourth. Unless I'm mistaken, neither you, Mabel nor you, Florence ever had that pleasure?"

Florence and I look at each other before we start laughing. "You don't have to add us to the list. Nor is it something either of us is likely to do in the future."

Myrtle announces, "I am off to visit Penny again today. I never know when she might be able to tell me what she thinks is so important. I also plan to talk with each of the residents in the rooms around her. They may also have seen something that might be important to the case. I just can't picture the police being patient with the residents who have dementia. Having dementia doesn't mean they couldn't have seen and taken note of things that they thought didn't fit their normal day. Penny always seemed so happy just to see me. The time may come when I would like to have someone do that for me."

Florence asks, "Myrtle, do you need to have one of us drop you off?"

"I've learned it's actually a fast bus trip. That will give me time to prepare myself. It's a nice Care Center, but it still breaks my heart there are so many women who aren't as lucky as we are. We form our own female care center right here." That thought makes all of us smile.

As my friends all head out my door, I realize Florence and I are the only two without a mission to accomplish. She reaches out to pat my arm. "I think you and I have earned the right to take ourselves to an early dinner. I have an idea that I'm not quite ready to share with the entire group, but I do want to run it past you. What sounds good for dinner tonight?"

We decide on the short walk to the Greek and Mediterranean restaurant that is in the downtown area. We rarely select it for our monthly Red Hat luncheons. Too many of the ladies declare that it is too spicy or that the food just doesn't agree with them. Florence and I are fortunate that we don't react that way. The walk feels just right after my afternoon nap. The walk back will probably also feel good after I stuff myself with pita bread and hummus.

As soon as the waiter has taken our orders, Florence takes a deep breath before looking me in the eye. "I've been taking another look at John and Elsie's accounts. After I got over the shock of how much he sent to that online church, I studied the pattern for which checks Elsie signed and those that John signed. Elsie signed checks for a year before putting John in the Care Center. Those checks were for the utilities. The back taxes on the house were paid from the proceeds of the sale as is customary. Once she moved from the house to the St. James, she only signed checks for that Care Center out of their joint account. She opened a personal account in her name only for her rent at the St. James."

"That matches with what she told me."

"What I noticed is that over the last two years, John continued to sign checks to his son and even more just for 'Cash.' He was no longer sending money to that church. More importantly, his handwriting and his signature changed remarkably. I don't think John wrote those checks. I also suspect he did not sign them. This continued even after John was in the Care Center."

"Are you saying that someone forged those checks?"

"I've taken the time to look closely at every check written in that time period. The check numbers I'm most concerned about are all from a different set of check blanks than the ones Elsie used. So yes, I am saying someone forged those checks. How do we get the police to take a good hard look at this?"

"I think I need to call Diana again."

Chapter Twenty-Six

During my walk the next morning, I concentrate more on how I might open the conversation with Diana than I do on my enjoyment of the birds sounds around me. I truly hate that my life is now revolving around how we can best take care of Elsie. A woman who spent years controlled by the men in her life should not have to have her friends put her in the same place. I can't imagine that Diana would ever have allowed a man to control her finances. I can only hope that she will be understanding when I place that call.

My phone is ringing as I try to unlock my door. I don't recognize the number, but it does appear to be a local one. I decide to answer hoping that it is not a telemarketer calling to tell me about Medicare plans I might qualify for. I've gotten very good at hanging up on those calls. "Hello?"

"Mabel Schmidel? This is Mark Emery. Thank you for answering even though I know you didn't recognize my number. I'm sure you are prepared for a telemarketer of some type. Ahhh - I hope you don't mind that I asked Elsie for your number."

"Mr. Emery, it is good to hear from you. Is there something I can help you with?"

"I am so out of practice at this; I feel like a sixteen-year-old boy asking a girl to go to the prom. I'm hoping I can take you to lunch or dinner this week. I want to get to know you better. I decided that asking you at John's Memorial was probably bad timing."

Wow! This is clearly not a telemarketer! I drop my keys, as I juggle my phone in shock. Now I need to say something intelligent. I need a moment. "Mark, please give me a minute. I was just unlocking my door after coming back from my morning walk. Let me get inside, so I can talk to you." Now I think I'm babbling. I pick up my keys, unlocked my door, and realized I really need to hit the bathroom before I can continue the conversation. "I'm inside, but give me a couple of more minutes." I don't wait for his answer. I put my phone on mute as I hurry into the bathroom. Mission accomplished, I guess it is time to say yes or no to the invitation. "Mark, are you still there?"

"I am. I realize I should have started the conversation by asking if you had a moment to talk. Forgive me if I startled you with my call."

I laugh. "I'm getting accustomed to receiving early morning calls about Elsie, but your call is definitely not one I was expecting. I should be free for lunch this week. When and where should I meet you?"

"Since I'm thinking of this as a date rather than a business meeting, how about I pick you up at your apartment building on Wednesday about noon? If you like seafood, I'm thinking Saltys might be a good choice. Will that work?"

A date? Oh dear! The man has to be a good ten years younger than I am if not more. I've not been on a date with a man in decades. Do I even know how to behave on a date? As Hattie would say, what the hell, why not? I don't seriously think he is a murder suspect, but this could give me a chance to learn a lot more that may help our investigation. "Saltys on Wednesday sounds good. Do you know where the St. James apartment building is?"

"Yes, it is not that far from my office. I look forward to Wednesday. Thank you. Until then, Mabel, take good care of yourself." I stand with my phone in my hand wondering what I'm getting myself into. *Lunch is one thing, but a date? Oh my.* To add to my distress, I may want to ask Diana and Elsie for a little more information about Mark Emery. He is still on our suspect list. How do I quiz them without telling them that I have agreed to a date?

It might be a good idea to let Diana know about my lunch plans with Mark without saying it is a date.

"Hi Diana, I hope it is not too early to call?"

"No, it isn't. I've been an early riser most of my life, and that hasn't changed in retirement. What is up?"

"I have some things to tell you about Elsie and some questions about Mark Emery that I'm hoping you can answer."

"I'm about to have my 2nd cup of coffee, and there is more in the pot if you would like to join me."

"I'll be there in a couple of minutes." I wonder if I should Google Mark or look for him on social media? At least then I would know the questions I want to ask Diana. Oh well, I can always decide to do that after she and I talk. It might be good to have some facts before Wednesday. If he tells me things that are not true about basic facts, we may want to investigate even more.

Diana hands me a cup of coffee and motions toward her living room. Because I don't wish to spill coffee everywhere, I park the cup on the coffee table before taking a seat on the sofa. Diana sits across from me and has a look of patience as she waits for me to ask my questions. I'll bet her law practice gave her lots of practice with that look. I take a sip of coffee to stall for just a moment. Do I tell her about Elsie or ask about Mark first? Mark may be easier, and it's not like we will forget about Elsie. "Mark Emery has asked me to have lunch with him on Wednesday. Because he was John's law partner, I said yes in hopes that we would learn something of value for our investigation. I would like to know more about him before then, and hoped you could help with that."

"My practice was in Seattle, and since Mark is here in Kent, I don't really know him personally all that well. I do know that his wife died about five years ago. I had heard that he had been thinking about retiring before she passed. He thought that retiring at seventy-five would give them time to do the things on their bucket list. Now he says that those things don't sound like as much fun to do by himself. He remarried, but that did not last very long. I'm not sure just what happened, but I think she may have been looking for a sugar daddy and he didn't want that job. Retiring on his eightieth birthday this year should still give him the time for a shortened bucket list. Are there specific things you wanted to know?"

"I would have put his age at much younger than seventy-nine! Some men seem to age much better than others. Hattie has learned that John mis-used funds from the law practice. Do you think Mark could still be angry about that?"

"If the rumors I had heard at the time were true, John could have been arrested. Mark stopped him before he could do too much damage. John's law license was revoked, he retired, and his malpractice insurance covered losses. Mark blamed the dementia rather than the man."

"Thank you for that. That will move him down in our suspect list, and I'll feel better about going to lunch with him."

"I'm hoping that lunch leads to a great connection between the two of you. I think you are just the kind of woman he could use in his life. Now, let's switch the conversation to Elsie. What have you learned that I need to know?"

"Florence believes the police should have a forensic accountant looking at signatures on checks from John and Elsie's accounts. She has serious concerns about who was signing the checks that Elsie did not sign."

"Before I call Stan, I have to ask one question. Is there any possibility that Mr. Johnson could have been the one to sign those checks?"

"From what Florence has said, there would be no way for Mr. Johnson to have done that. The issue with these checks starts before Elsie moved into the St. James.

There really doesn't appear to have any connection between Elsie and Mr. Johnson until she moved here. Even then, they didn't start dating until three months ago."

"I'll call Stan, and then I will let you know what the result is."

"Thank you." I wish I could also remove Mark Emery as a suspect with the checks as easily as I can Mr. Johnson.

Chapter Twenty-Seven

Myrtle and I decide it is a good day to visit Penny. I do not have high hopes that she will be able to tell us whatever it is she thinks is important. We will expand our chats to include two or three of the residents on either side of John's old room. Myrtle admits that she had not been successful in chatting with those residents in her prior visits. Today, she will focus on Penny while I try the other residents. We really need to follow up with Hattie and the investigations at the Care Center. I would hate to have a staff member there be the killer, but at least that would end this nightmare for Mr. Johnson and Elsie.

We meet in the lobby to button up our raincoats and get our umbrellas ready. I love living in the Seattle area, but when it turns into Pacific North Wet, it becomes a challenge. Before we can head out the door, Hattie comes in looking like a very colorful drowned rat. At least the colors from her Mohawk aren't running down her face. Her lime green T-shirt would qualify her for a wet T-shirt competition. Even her orange sneakers squish water as she walks over to where we are standing. It is a struggle not to laugh. "Oh Hattie, is there any part of you that is not wet?"

"It wasn't raining when I headed out this morning. Now even my leak proof panties are wet. Hopefully the things I learned will make it worthwhile. I have discovered where the night nursing staff likes to go for breakfast after their shift ends which is easier on my liver than meeting the day staff for drinks. I hoped to get an update about the Care Center. I did learn there appears to be a suspicious pattern to deaths in the memory ward going back almost a year. The investigation into that pattern had started before John's death. They thought it had ended when one of the aides had quit to work in another center. Now they are reevaluating those deaths as well as John's. I don't have any additional details, but we might need to add another suspect to our list. Now I really need to change clothes. You might need boots to go with those raincoats. We are having serious rain rather than our normal drizzle."

Maybe we will learn more during our time at the Care Center. Hopefully Penny will finally tell us what she knows.

My luck has run out. I knew this day would come, and I am prepared. I still feel guilty about the lies I told before, but I can continue now with the truth. On each of my prior visits I had not encountered Crystal, the administrator. Today she is at the desk where we need to sign in for the memory ward. I paste a big smile on my face before turning to Myrtle. "Myrtle, I don't think you have had a chance to meet Ms. Stratton. She is the administrator here that I met with about my sister Eunice." I do hope Myrtle remembers that I had used Eunice as a reason to make my first visit here.

Myrtle also pastes on a smile as she extends her hand to Crystal. "I'm Myrtle Anderson Bailey, Penny's old friend. It's very nice to make your acquaintance."

"I'm delighted to meet you, Myrtle. Penny has been so happy that the two of you have come to visit so often. Have you actually been able to determine that she is the Penny you knew growing up?"

It is Myrtle's turn to tell Crystal a lie. "It has been a challenge because Penny's memory comes and goes so quickly. We keep hoping that we will learn enough about her to know that for sure." In reality, Myrtle had confirmed that this was not the woman who had once been her friend. She had learned that Penny had not gone to the same high school, although they may have met at some time during those high school years.

"That can be very difficult. Mabel, I had wanted to follow up. Have you and your sister made a decision about her plans?"

This time I get to tell the truth even though that decision had been made five years ago. "My niece and I agreed that having her in a care center in Portland makes the most sense. We hope that having her daughter and grandchildren close will give her memory a boost. I can easily catch the train to make monthly visits." I only feel a little bit guilty about saying it was memory issues for Eunice. It was her two strokes that had necessitated moving her to a nursing home. She wasn't there long before a third stroke took her life.

We waited patiently as Crystal used the pin pad to unlock the door. Penny as always is waiting just inside. Crystal pats her shoulder before returning to the desk. I hold my breath as Penny starts to speak. "Myrtle, I see you've brought your friend. Is it okay if I share with her what I wanted to tell you about John? I'm afraid I'll lose my thought if I wait until it is just the two of us."

I suck in a quick breath before holding it again. Myrtle says, "You can tell both of us."

"A man came to see John just after Elsie left on the day he died."

Oh my goodness, this is what we've been waiting to hear! I don't wait for Myrtle to respond. "Did you know the man? Had he been to see John before?"

"Who are you? And what man are you talking about?"

We now have a clue, but only a small clue. Unfortunately, this information still keeps Mr. Johnson on the suspect list.

Chapter Twenty-Eight

Staring at my image in the mirror is not going to change the conclusion I had reached an hour ago. Changing my dress three times does not make this outfit any more comfortable than the first one had been, but it really has nothing to do with the dress. A woman of 86 years should not be getting ready for a date. I really need to just think of this as nothing more than a lunch with a new friend. If he cares about how I'm dressed, we won't be friends for long.

As I pace from one end of my apartment to the other, I can't decide which scenario is worse. If I spend the next fifteen minutes pacing in the lobby, my friends will notice and ask me what is going on. If I stay here to do my pacing, my friends will hear the door open after Mark buzzes for access. They will have enough time to drill him before I can reach the lobby. Oh why, why did I consent for him to pick me up here? I wish I had thought to get his cell number. I could have asked him to call me just before he arrived. He has always called me from his office which is no help right now. I don't even know if he is a punctual individual. I continue to pace for another five minutes when I have what I consider a flash of brilliance. I can go down to sit in my car where I can watch the front walkway. I can pretend that I have just gotten back to the apartment building to intercept him before he reaches the door. I can actually breathe as I take the elevator to the lobby. That ends as the elevator doors open, and I see Mark ready to push the buzzer for my apartment. I can only hope that none of the residents on the first floor will hear that sound prior to me reaching the front door.

I hear the buzzer before I am half way across the lobby. As I open the door, I see Betty peeking out from her door. I know there will be questions later. "Hi Mark, you're right on time." Mark puts a hand on each of my shoulders to pull me in for a quick kiss on my cheek. Betty will have that news to everyone long before I get back from lunch.

The door hasn't closed yet when Mark makes this even worse. "Mabel, you look gorgeous." Agreeing to this lunch may not have been my best decision. I don't know if the look I give him is a smile or grimace as he tucks my arm into his. He pats my hand as he leads me to his car. Of course, the man doesn't drive a little import car. I'll take this as a sign that he is not going through a midlife crisis. His car is a large black Mercedes that smells like new leather as he opens the passenger door. At least there is lots of room to put my butt in the seat before swinging my long legs in as gracefully as I manage. I hadn't even noticed that the car had started before Mark had opened my door. I am expecting the roar from a powerful engine, but the engine sounds more like a cat purring. Mark's seat adjusts as soon as he puts his hands on the steering wheel. He checks his mirror before pulling out of our parking lot. "Let me know if I have the temperature set correctly for you. This model also has the massaging seats. I thought it would be a nice feature on a long trip although I've yet to use it."

"I assume this is an electric vehicle. I thought about buying one, but it would need to be a hybrid because a plug-in would not be an option at the St. James Apartments."

"I had similar concerns about how far I could drive between plug-ins. I plan to do a lot of travel over the next few years. At this time, it will take a little more planning, but the technology is advancing quickly. Do you like to travel?"

Electric cars and travel should be safe topics without getting too personal during this lunch. I remember friends telling me to never bring up your late husband when talking with a man. That had been shortly after George had passed, and I had zero interest in talking with any strange man. I wonder if bringing him up now will put the brakes on whatever this relationship is. Is that what I want to do? I'm not certain, but this will be a good time to find out. "My late husband George and I had plans to travel after he retired. He died from a heart attack before we could do many of those things. We did do a transatlantic cruise, but I really haven't done much traveling by myself." Oh dear, does that sound like I'm asking for a travel partner?

"When my ex-wife had announced that she thought travel was a waste of good money, I knew something would need to change if I were going to enjoy my retirement years. That is not the reason we are divorced, but did add to it. That would be a required shared interest for any partner I would want in the future."

If I bring up topics about travel now, will that make me sound like I'm applying for that position? Not even talking that cruise is a good idea now. I do hope I can find safe things to say or this may be a very challenging lunch. I may need to focus the conversation on Mark's relationship with John. I may not want to be Mark's travel buddy, but I would like to remove him as a suspect. Should I turn the conversation to helping us with the investigation?

I'm glad I took some time on my appearance. Salty's isn't a fancy restaurant, but it is a very popular one right on Puget Sound. Mark and I both order the crab and shrimp Louie. My first thought had been to order the chowder, but Mark had pointed out the combination on the salad. I decide I'd live a little since this is a date. A $10 chowder rather than a $25 salad might have made me look like I was trying to be a cheap date. Ordering almost anything else on the menu would still make me feel like a gold digger. When did lunch get so expensive? Mark orders a nice white wine. I almost start to relax, but I still need to ask questions.

"You and John were partners in your firm for a long time, until Elsie said it all fell apart. I assume it was due to

John's advancing dementia. That must have been so hard. How did you handle it?" Hopefully that isn't too much to ask.

"It wasn't the best time I've ever had. It was so sad to watch the changes in a man I had considered a friend for so long. Elsie was a big help. It could have been much worse, but we caught things in time. I tried hard to keep the details from spreading throughout the legal community, but some things did get out. All of that is ancient history. Tell me about you. How did a beautiful woman like you end up in an apartment building filled with old women."

I take a big bite of my salad to give me a few more seconds before I respond. This lunch is not going the way I hoped. "Actually, I love my friends there. It has been the perfect place to live after selling my house." I decide to ignore the comment about being beautiful. That just sounds like so much BS. "Where do you live?" Maybe I'll get some information to add to our investigation yet.

I would never admit to anyone how much I enjoyed lunch. Mark seemed to stop trying so hard. Maybe he picked up that his complements made me uncomfortable. It is hard to not enjoy good food, an expansive view of Puget Sound, and a chat with a man who makes me laugh. If this is what dating at eighty-six is really like, it may not be so bad after all.

Chapter Twenty-Nine

I manage to slip into the apartment building without seeing a single door open in the lobby. I cross my fingers that that will not change as I push the elevator button for the fifth floor. I am sure that Betty has sent out the alarm that I was meeting a man who kissed my cheek. It is past time for our investigative team to meet; I might as well address both issues at once. I send out the text messages to meet at my apartment at 3 o'clock. Hopefully we will have information that can push our investigation forward. At the very least we can list what we know about all of our possible suspects, and I can nip the gossip in the bud.

As I change into my comfy jeans and a colorful tunic top, I take a moment to glance at the clock. Good grief, did we really spend two and a half hours over lunch? I quickly move to the kitchen to fill the teakettle and make a pot of coffee. My friends will be at the door in minutes. I should have pushed the meeting off until four to give me time to think up an explanation for Mark. When in doubt, go for the truth, without saying the lunch was a date.

Betty and Hattie march in to my apartment the second I open the door. My first thought was two horses neck-and-neck racing toward the finish line. Betty stops abruptly to shake her finger in my face. "I do hope you are prepared to answer my questions."

Betty and Hattie are followed closely by Florence and Ethel just as Diana steps out of the elevator. All of these ladies have very determined looks on their faces. Either we have learned things about our investigation, or Betty has sent out gossip about my lunch. I must remember to call it a luncheon and not a date. I really need to present it as a business meeting that happened to be over lunch.

As soon as I close the door, Betty puts on her very best teacher voice that I'm sure can be heard two blocks down the street, "Mabel Schmidel, who was that man who came to pick you up, and why was he kissing you?"

Hattie turns toward me with a look of shock on her face. "You have a man kissing you?"

Betty puts her hands on her hips, "Hush Hattie. I asked first so she has to answer me." Her look of determination made me realize there was no way I could dodge her questions. "I know you heard me, Mabel, and I expect an answer."

"He wasn't really kissing me. He gave me a quick greeting kiss on my cheek." I try for a little humor, "That's my story and I'm sticking to it." All of the women just stare at me. Betty now folds her arms across her chest. I would normally say they were folded under her boobs, but her action clearly demonstrates she doesn't have any. I try very hard to focus on what I say next. "You have all seen him. That was John and Elsie's attorney, Mark Emery who was at John's Memorial. Diana had talked with him. I met him when I went with Elsie for the reading of the will."

Hattie was almost as loud as Betty normally is, "So now we know who he was, but we don't know why he was greeting you. Did you leave with him? Where did you go? He is on our suspect list. Was it really safe for you to be alone with him?"

"We went to Salty's for a luncheon. I thought it would be the best way to get information for our investigation. I really don't think he was involved. John's malpractice insurance had covered the money that he misused. Mark had no reason to hold a grudge against John." I could feel my neck and face start to warm. I am too old to blush over a man. I take a quick sip of my tea. "Wow!" As I fan my face, "This tea was hotter than I realized." I cross my fingers in hopes that my friends accept that reason for my flushed face. "Now let's focus on what we know about our investigation."

Diana is the first to speak, "I can confirm that John's insurance covered the loss to the practice. Mark has a very good reputation. I really can't envision that he would have any reason to harm John." She gives me a shy smile, and then a thumbs up that only I can see. I try to keep my blush under control.

Betty squints her eyes a bit as she looks at me, but she doesn't say anything. Hattie, however, does, "Luncheon? Like hell! You had a date with a good-looking man and don't want to share the details. That's not fair. I'm always willing to tell you about any man I meet."

I almost feel guilty, not quite, but almost. Hattie pats my shoulder as she turns to the group. "Moving on, I can announce that the Care Center believes that any issues they may have had with deaths there ended when they fired one of the orderlies." That strikes me as a story that needs to be checked, but it is not our concern right now.

Betty pulls the whiteboard close and uses the correct colored marker to add that information to our suspects list. Ethel looks almost smug as she announces, "Whatever you said to Stan, Diana, must have worked. A forensic accountant has started looking at the issues with the accounts Florence identified. Maybe soon we will know who wrote the checks and where that money went." I silently hope that Mr. Johnson and Elsie had nothing to do with the money. Diana just nods her head.

Myrtle turns to me, "Mabel can you come with me to the Care Center tomorrow? I never know what Penny may say, but I'm hoping that we can interview all of the people who live around her. If she thinks she saw someone in John's room surely someone else did as well."

"Let's plan to go right after my morning walk. Penny does seem to be more alert first thing in the morning. The same may be true of her neighbors. If we learn anything, we can plan another meeting for the day after tomorrow."

Chapter Thirty

I am still so full from my lunch with Mark that I decide to fix some of my frozen homemade soup for dinner. My soup always tastes so much better, and I know is healthier than any I could get from a can. The warm soup is a perfect match for the warmth that I feel just thinking about that lunch. I haven't felt this way in a long time. I've had men make a pass even in the years since George has died. They always made me feel dirty. I would want a hot shower to wash away the contact with them. Mark makes me feel warm, safe, and feminine. That is not an easy way to feel for an eighty-six-year-old woman. My thoughts are interrupted by my phone. I don't even take the time to glance at the number before I answer. "Hello?"

"Good evening, Mabel. I hope I didn't interrupt your dinner?"

"Mark! I wasn't expecting your call. I just finished eating, and you're not interrupting at all."

"Good, good. I'm glad I'm not, but dinner is exactly why I wanted to call. I so enjoyed our lunch that I wanted to ask you to dinner. Tomorrow night might make me look a little pushy, so are you available two nights from now?"

I take a deep breath. I don't know what surprises me the most, that he called tonight or that he wants to take me to dinner so soon. I'm also surprised by how delighted I am to hear his voice. There is no question in my mind. "I also enjoyed our lunch and would love to have dinner with you." My thoughts immediately go to all of those dresses I tried on and rejected. This might be the time to call Claire for a shopping trip.

"Wonderful! This will give me time to select a special restaurant for a very special lady. Will 6 o'clock work for you?"

"That would be perfect. I look forward to seeing you then. Good night, Mark."

"Until then. Good night, Mabel." This call leaves me with a very tingly feeling.

I hang up and immediately dial Claire before I change my mind. "Hi Claire, I'm calling to ask for a favor. Can you go shopping with me tomorrow?"

"Of course. Are you shopping for something special?"

"I remember when you told me about you and your friends shopping for fancy undies. I want some things that make me proud to be a woman. I also want a dress for an upcoming dinner date."

I hear Claire trying hard to suppress her giggle. "Good for you. I'm delighted to help you find just the right things. How about I pick you up about 2 o'clock tomorrow?"

"Thank you. I'll see you then."

"Just be prepared, I'll want all of the juicy details after this date."

"I'm not sure about the juicy part, but I promise to share the details. You are the perfect friend for that!"

When I was growing up, I was the only daughter among my mother's group of friends. They often would invite me to go with one or another of them on a day's adventure. This normally included shopping, but sometimes it was to an art gallery or museum. They said they enjoyed my enthusiasm, and I thought I had the greatest group of aunts in the entire world.

Going shopping with Claire will bring that feeling of enthusiasm I so need for this adventure. My friends from the St. James would make me feel embarrassed rather than excited. I'm buying fancy undies not because I believe Mark will see them, but because I want to feel more feminine than my every day granny panties offer. There has always been a place for underwear that is comfortable in plain white cotton. For dinner with Mark, I don't want to be uncomfortable, but knowing there's a bit of lace and satin should help keep a smile on my face. I realize that for the last 20+ years I've been content looking a little dowdy around the edges. That ends tomorrow. I have no way of knowing how many more years I will have, but starting now, I truly want them to be fun years. In my heart I know George would approve.

Chapter Thirty-One

As I drive Myrtle to the Care Center, I keep thinking that we have not been very good detectives. I know that Jessica Fletcher would do reenactments as she wrote her stories in Murder She Wrote©. Our early discussions about the murder were the same as a reenactment. That was when we concluded that Elsie was neither tall enough nor strong enough to have used a pillow to smother John. Since then, we have used gossip as a way of learning what was happening at the Care Center and in the police investigation. We know that the residents of the Care Center may not be the best eyewitnesses, but surely there is a way to help them share what they know. "Myrtle, do you think we would have better luck if we had a photo array of men to show Penny and her neighbors?"

"That might be a good idea since even if they saw someone, they may not know the man's name. We would probably want more than just a head shot to work with. I'm sure Elsie has pictures of John with his son, but how do we get pictures of Mr. Johnson and your friend Mark to add to that array?"

"Diana may know about a social media post that would work for Mark. Mr. Johnson may present a bigger issue. We would have to take a picture without him knowing, because I really don't want to explain what we're doing. We will also want to add John's son-in-law to that photo group. I wonder if Elsie might also have pictures of him?"

"Let's continue with our plan to talk with Penny and her neighbors today. It will take us a while to collect all of those photos. I do hope that Penny's having a good day, but even if she's not, I know she looks forward to our visits. We are so fortunate that we know where we live, and on most days can even remember what we had for breakfast."

I have to laugh because Myrtle really does have a point. The residents of the St. James are very lucky. In the years I've lived there, we have not had anyone die nor has anyone had to relocate to a nursing home. One resident got married and moved into a house with her new husband. Two moved in with children and two others shocked everyone when they decided to share one apartment. Despite the gossip, I did not really care if they had two beds or only one.

The notebook with the usual sign-in sheets is on the desk in its usual place, but there are no staff members visible. I make a quick decision, "Myrtle, give me a signal if anyone is heading our direction." I open the notebook to today's sign-in sheet. I start to skim through much older pages. I want to see how often Elsie was here to visit her husband and how often her stepson visited his father. I find Elsie signature two months before John's death. A few pages later I also see that John's daughter has signed in as well as Brett. It appears the daughter would visit once a week and he did every other week. It looks like neither of them stayed more than about ten minutes. Elsie consistently stayed for a full hour. The pages for the two weeks before John's death are missing. I assume the police have taken those pages. Myrtle gives me a quick elbow in my ribs. I look up to see one of the nurses heading our direction. I pick up the pen as I turn the pages back to today's before signing in. I turned to Myrtle as I hand her the pen, "Your turn."

The nurse is one we have met here before. "Good morning, ladies. You need access to the memory wing, correct?"

"Yes, we are here to see our friend Penny. We are hoping this will be a good day for her." As I watch the nurse punch in the four - digit code for access, I wonder how often that code is changed. I've seen the nurses and aides use the pin pad, but my mind is usually somewhere else. I am sure the police have asked how often it is changed, but I think it might be very important for our investigation. I'll have to check with Hattie to see if that is information, she has picked up yet.

Penny is waiting in her regular spot just inside the doors. She claps her hands, "Visiting day makes me so happy! It is wonderful to see both of you." She turns her wheelchair to start down the hall toward her room.

The nurse calls out before she closes the door, "In case you don't spot anyone in this wing when you are ready to leave, just use the buzzer above the keypad so we can open the door for you."

Others had pointed out that buzzer on our past visits. Today I take the time for a close look at the exit keypad. I've never had the time to do that with the keypad for entrance. Four of the keys are more worn than the others. I would not be able to determine in what order the keys are pressed, but that might be something that I could watch for the next time we enter. Because the four numbers are in sequence, it might not be hard to guess. This could very well be how the killer entered and exited without any staff members knowing. I am glad I really am not looking for a place for my late sister Eunice. This facility no longer appears to be as secure as I would want for one of my family members.

Penny starts into happy chatter about her high school days. Myrtle and I offer our support with laughter and head nods. She becomes quite animated with tales about Mrs. McCall and the essays that had been read in that English class. Suddenly Penny looks sadly at Myrtle. "I had dreamed of being a writer, but I never did. My dreams for my future never included being forced to live here. I am envious that you two can come and go as you please." Her words bring tears to my eyes. Myrtle must be feeling the same as she reaches out and gives Penny a hug. I look around the room for the box of tissues. I pull out three, one for each of us. Myrtle and I both wipe our eyes. After she blows her nose, Penny gets very quiet. It only takes a minute before she has fallen asleep. The emotions must have worn her out. It is time for us to introduce ourselves to her neighbors.

Chapter Thirty-Two

On our drive back to the St. James, Myrtle and I talk about what we didn't learn from any of Penny's neighbors. We agree that pictures might help with at least some of those neighbors. It was hard to attempt to talk with those who just stared off into space. My sister Eunice may have suffered from the effects of her strokes, but she knew who she was and who we were to the very end. I tell Myrtle that I have things to take care of this afternoon. I don't want to tell her about my shopping trip with Claire. I am pleased when Myrtle volunteers to talk with Elsie about the pictures we need. I should have time to call Diana about pictures of Mark before Claire arrives.

When Claire had lived next door to me at the St. James, all of the residents considered her a breath of fresh air. The thirty-year age difference made me very aware that I have become an old woman. At the same time her enthusiasm renews my joy in living every day. I also know I can trust her honesty with my shopping trip today. The last thing she would want would be to make me feel foolish. In addition, her friendship, despite the age difference, is a reminder that there is no reason I can't have a relationship with a man who is significantly younger than I am. At least Mark is not Claire's age which would be almost scandalous.

Precisely at two I'm startled by a knock on my door. *Oh dear, this is not a good time for one of my friends to drop in unannounced for a chat.* I am more than surprised to discover Claire in my doorway. "Darling, I was expecting you to buzz from the lobby. Come in while I grab my purse. It is so good to see you." I give her a quick hug.

"I came a little bit early to check in with my mother-in-law. I am so happy that Florence is your neighbor. I thought you might want to keep this shopping trip between just us. As expected, Betty was right there when I came in the front door. She reminds me of a little bulldog guarding access." That description makes me laugh, because it is absolutely correct. Some of our residents might be described in terms of cats for a variety of reasons, but Betty is clearly a watch dog. She is too tiny to resemble a German shepherd or other type of junkyard dog, but she is a wonderful watch dog. "I even parked in the back lot so she could not see when we both get in my car. If she sees us leaving together, she will just assume I ended my visit and you are off for a walk."

I give Claire another quick hug, "I do so love you. You really should be a member of our St. James detectives." I turn off the lights and lock my door while Claire pushes the button for the elevator. May this adventure begin.

Claire has barely turned out of the parking lot before she gives me a very intense look. "I seriously doubt if this shopping trip has anything to do with the St. James detectives. That is a cute name for you ladies, by the way. A shopping trip of this nature always means a man. I can't say I was expecting that, but I will say, good for you! Now I want all of the details, but even more I want all the details after the clothing items we buy work their magic. Let's start with his name, and go from there.

I take a deep breath. I have expected her to ask questions. This is part of the reason I found it hard to sleep last night. Thinking about what may happen on a dinner date with Mark did not make sleeping any easier. "His name is Mark Emery. He is an attorney I met as part of this investigation. Actually, he was one of John's business partners as well as the one who conducted the reading of John's will that I attended with Elsie. I really can't give you the details that I'm sure you would like to have. I may know more after this dinner date."

"What I really want to know is if his kisses curl your toes, but I'm willing to wait to hear all about that." I can only shake my head. In the mall Claire leads me directly to the Gilly Hicks™ store which has replaced Victoria Secret™. She doesn't stop until she is in front of the colorful display of thong panties. She selects a lacy pair in hot pink before turning in my direction. I am again shaking my head, but for an entirely different reason.

"I'm looking for something that will make me feel more feminine not uncomfortable." I turn in a circle to take in the displays of thongs, push-up bras and see-through teddies. "I'm not sure I'll find anything here that will do that for me."

Claire loops her arm through mine, and says, "I didn't think this was exactly what you had in mind, but thought it would be easier to make good selections once we knew what you clearly did not want. Where would you like to head next?"

We proceed down the mall to Macy's™ where I find attractive but more age-appropriate underwear and two dresses that neatly fill the bill as date dresses. One is in a simple cotton tropical print shirt waist and the second is a blue wrap jersey that actually feels like I'm wearing a T-shirt. The styling, however, makes it dressy rather than casual. As we drive back to the St. James, I silently ask myself why I felt the need to buy more than one date dress. *Am I expecting more than just one dinner with Mark?*

Chapter Thirty-Three

I recently read about a Dutch supermarket that has a special checkout lane. Rather than the fast, and usually self-check lane that is found in US markets, this one is a slow check. It is designed for customers who wish to chat with the checker. I had two thoughts simultaneously as I read the article. The first was that most of that chat was likely to be gossip. The second was that type of checkout would not be necessary for the residents at the St. James. In an apartment building filled with women, there is always someone to talk with, and undoubtedly that talk would be gossip. I decide that the best way to limit the gossip after Claire drops me at my car will be to move my purchases from the Macy's bags to Walmart ones. Shopping at Macy's would require explanation where Walmart does not. I also realize that our investigation needs to shift from gossip to facts if we are going to help Elsie and Mr. Johnson. It is clearly time to call an investigation meeting. If I call the meeting for before my dinner date, I can share that announcement as part of the investigation. That might keep the gossip to a minimum. At least I can try.

Myrtle is first to start off the meeting, "Mabel and I have been to the Care Center so often I'm starting to feel like we live there. This time we talked with all of Penny's neighbors. Other than getting offers to participate in activities I hadn't thought about in years, we really didn't learn anything new. We might have better luck if we go back with pictures of all of our suspects."

Hattie starts laughing, "If you think any of those invitations might be from men who could follow through, let me know!" By now the entire group is laughing except for Betty. She taps on her teacup with one of the markers as she gives us all a frown. I can just imagine how she would've treated disruptive students.

I decide this might not be the moment to share the news about my dinner plans. "I took the time to study the keypad that opens the door in that section of the Care Center. The entrance keypad appears to be cleaner than that for the exit one. Although it is possible that they may reorder the same four numbers, I know what four numbers are used by the dirt on that keypad. It would not take many observations as the numbers are keyed in to guess their order. My first thought had been there might be hundreds of combinations, but the Internet says there actually only twenty-four if none of the numbers can be entered more than once. I don't know if the system would allow you to guess before locking someone out. I know my bank gets nasty if I can't remember my password to login after three tries."

Myrtle looks at me with alarm, "That really does not sound like something I would want to try. I don't want one of the nurses thinking that we are trying to escape rather than being visitors!"

Laughter erupts again. Hattie looks more pensive as she says, "I'll have to think about a way to ask that of the nurses. It might be a difficult topic to work into a general conversation. It does sound like it would not be easy for a stranger to exit that ward without being escorted by a nurse. Whoever killed John had to know how to enter and leave easily."

"That has been my thought as well. Now how do we get a picture of Mr. Johnson as well as our other suspects?"

"I can ask Elsie," Ethel says. "I'm sure John had pictures of his son and son-in-law. I honestly don't think Elsie would have thrown those out. It's past time I spent some time with her as well. Mr. Johnson might be a bit harder. Is there a website or Facebook page about the St.

James? I've never thought to look. Would Terry have a picture there of Mr. Johnson?"

Florence says, "I've never thought about that either. I'll call Terry after we finish here. If he doesn't have that, I will suggest it. A woman coming to look at an apartment might want to know that she is actually talking to the manager. A picture on a website might address that."

This might be my chance to share my dinner plans, "I've agreed to have dinner with Mark, John's former partner, but I really can't see being able to snap a picture of him. I might have better luck searching on the Internet. Surely his picture is on the company website. I do plan to ask him about any visits he may have made to John in the Care Center."

Betty squints at me, "Mabel Schmidel, don't try to fool us. You having a date with Mark has nothing to do with our investigation."

"Our investigation is extremely important to both Elsie and Mr. Johnson. Agreeing to dinner seems like the best way to get as much information as I can." I hope that I have truly used a stern tone. Just calling this a dinner date still causes butterflies in my stomach. "I will let you know tomorrow if I learn anything of value." Hattie gives me a smile that goes from ear to ear, while Myrtle gives me a wink. Who do I think I'm fooling?

Chapter Thirty-Four

When I jump at the sound of the outside door buzzer, I realize how nervous I am. I quickly pick up my purse and sweater before buzzing the door access to allow Mark into the lobby. I really don't want him to loiter there too long. Betty seems to hear every time that door opens, and she has been known to ask very rude questions. I can only hope that she isn't listening at her door when I step out of the elevator to see the smile on Mark's face. "The blue of that dress becomes you. You look lovely."

I feel almost tongue-tied knowing that I am blushing, "Thank you. Shall we go?" Why does this man make me feel like I'm a teenager? I see Betty's door open just a crack as we walk out of the lobby. I am glad that I told my friends that I was going to dinner with Mark. Hopefully, Betty won't make up some fantasy about how he greeted me. The truth will be bad enough. *Why did I ever agree to this*?

Mark holds the car door for me as I try to remember how to be graceful as I swing in my legs. The feeling of the butter soft leather seats has me thinking about the comparison of my little import car to this luxury model. I've been quite content with my little car, but I almost feel sorry for it now. I try not to giggle as the thought pops into my head that comparing the two cars is similar to comparing my plain cotton granny panties with the satin and lace pair I'm wearing tonight. There is a time and place for each.

Mark's voice interrupts my comparison. "When was the last time you have been to the Tacoma Art Museum?"

I take a moment to think before I answer. "It is been a couple of years since I have been to the Seattle Art

Museum, but I don't think I've ever been to the one in Tacoma. Is there a special reason that you're asking?"

"I thought it might be enjoyable to view the museum before we go to dinner. There is an exhibit there I want to see before it moves on. I should also have asked if you like Japanese food before I made reservations. The restaurant I selected is only a block away from the museum. I thought it would make a nice walk, if we are not both too tired after the museum."

"I can honestly say I've eaten very little Japanese food, but I am more than open to trying it. As for walking that is something I try to do as often during the day as I can. Most days I start my morning with a walk to the park that is near the apartment building."

"That sounds like a wonderful way to start the day and get more exercise. Now that I'm semi-retired, I feel the need to do that more than I did while I was working full time. I can't say I get excited about going to a gym. Maybe some morning soon I could join you for a walk? I enjoy your company, but don't want to appear too pushy."

Do I consent to that idea, or wait until after this dinner date? I decide to give a non-commitment answer, "That might be nice."

Mark skillfully pulls his car into the museum parking lot. He parks in a slot marked reserved for Board Directors. I can guess that his active involvement is how he knows all about the exhibit he wants to see. If he is a serious art critic, my responses may not match his expectations. I know what I like, but I would never consider my opinions that of a critic. I may not need that second date dress after all. This evening may dramatize our differences as much as the seats in our individual cars.

When the young lady at the reception desk greets Mark by name, I realize he is actively involved and not just a name on a list of board members. I am even more shocked when he says, "Cindy, this is my friend Mabel

Schmidel. Would you please add her name as my designated guest." He then turns his attention toward me. "As my designated guest, you can come to the museum anytime you wish as a VIP member."

Oh golly; I hope I give the correct responses as we look at the exhibit he wants to see. "That is very thoughtful of you." *I feel like I should say more, but this might be a good time to just smile and keep my mouth shut.* Mark takes my hand as he leads me down the hall and into the exhibit. I'm immediately struck by the walls covered with paintings in vivid colors and swirling shapes. *How am I ever going to be able to say anything intelligent about these paintings?*

As we stop in front of the first painting, I read the plaque beside it. This work is titled 'His Royal Majesty' and dated '2010.' I assume this means that the exhibit will show a progression of the artist's work over time. I notice that Mark is looking at me rather than at the painting. I turn my attention back to the painting. As if by magic, the random brightly colored swirls take shape as a cat sitting on a cushion. I can't keep the tone of surprise out of my voice, "Why did I only see colored swirls, but now clearly see a cat?"

"This is why I wanted to see this exhibit in person. 'Magic' is often used when critics describe this artist's work. Maybe we can figure out how she does this. By the way, I never asked if you like cats."

"One of my friends in our apartment building has a cat that we take turns enjoying for a day. We all spoil that cat rotten, but as owner, she gets the litter box!"

"Besides talking about what we see here tonight, I will tell you stories about my cat over our dinner. Shall we move on?"

Chapter Thirty-Five

The art exhibit is even more fascinating than I had expected. Each painting of shapes and vivid colors held objects of mystery that only revealed themselves once a person stopped to study what was in front of them. I have no idea how the artist created that magic, but I am a fan. As Mark and I walk the short block to the restaurant, we continue our discussion about the paintings. We then talk about other museums and other paintings that he has enjoyed over the years.

I'm not sure exactly what I had been expecting of a Japanese restaurant, but it was definitely not the contemporary feel of this one. It is light and bright and airy, clearly not like some of the Chinese restaurants I have been to with black lacquer furniture and red lanterns everywhere. The menu is in English, but I have no idea what to expect from any one of the dishes. I am quite happy to let Mark order for the two of us. He does so quickly before turning his full attention toward me. He has a very casual tone in his voice as he reaches out to take my hand, "I did not expect that you would be content to have anyone other than yourself in control. You strike me as a very strong woman, Mabel Schmidel. It is been a long time since I've had a woman who fascinates me in the way you do."

I feel myself blushing again. I honestly have no idea what to say. I am torn between needing information for our investigation, and enjoying time with this man who sparks my interest. As I struggle with my answer, I am saved by our server who places first small plates and then a larger dish of what I recognize as sushi on the table in front of us. Some of the pieces of sushi are topped with what is clearly raw fish. I must have a surprise look on my face, because Mark laughs. "I thought we would start with a mixture of sushi and nigiri. If you have not eaten Japanese food before, I thought sashimi might be a little too much."

"What is sashimi?"

"Oh, that is delicate raw fish or raw meat. It is served plain, as opposed to nigiri which is served on rice and topped with rice vinegar."

"I recognize sushi, but I've never actually eaten it. I'm willing to give all of it a try."

Mark gives me a big smile as he says, "In Japan we would place a small dab of wasabi on top before gently dipping in soy sauce. I find it easier to mix the wasabi with the soy sauce before dipping. The hit of horseradish can be shocking, and mixing it helps dilute it. Would you like me to fix your plate?"

I nod my head, and watch carefully as Mark uses his chopsticks to mix the green paste that I assume must be the wasabi with soy sauce before putting three pieces of sushi and one of the nigiri on my plate. He prepares the same on his plate. At least I know how to hold my chopsticks as I watch him pick up and then dip his nigiri before taking a bite of it. I do the same. "I can taste the horseradish and can understand why it needs to be diluted." I take a second bite of the nigiri without a second dip in the wasabi-soy sauce mixture. "Is this raw salmon?"

"It is. Are you ready to try the Ahi tuna? This other one is yellowtail."

"All of this is a new adventure, so I'm willing to sample it. Have you been to Japan?"

"Actually, I was there on a short trip when John was killed. I have friends that I normally meet in Hawaii, but they were unable to travel and I decided to meet them there. Because of the extended travel time my five-day trip meant I only was in Japan for three days. Maybe in the future you and I can plan to see more of the country together."

By now we have finished the plate of sushi and nigiri. I don't have to answer Mark before the server places larger plates and then many bowls of food on the table. "This looks wonderful. Will you tell me what I'm eating with each of these dishes?"

I give Mark a big smile as he answers, "Of course. Do you want to start with a small spoonful of each? I do like that they serve the entrées with spoons rather than expecting us to use our chopsticks to place the food on our plates. That will not be true in Japan." I have gotten the information I needed for our investigation without having to ask. I can spend the rest of dinner asking more questions about traveling in Japan.

Chapter Thirty-Six

Each member of our investigative team marches into my apartment with the same frown on her face. I have never known them to be absolutely silent as they take their seats around my table. Not even one reaches for a cup nor the teapots that I have already placed there. It was clearly not my imagination that Betty saw me when I came home last night. I do not have long to wait before Betty turns her teacher face on me as she starts in in her teacher voice. "Mabel Schmidel, what were you thinking letting a murder suspect kiss you like that? We're not talking about a simple cheek kiss. We are talking one of those open mouth French kisses straight out of a romance novel!"

After tossing and turning most of the night, I'm still not sure what had me worked up the most. That kiss had my toes curling in a way I had never expected I would experience again after dear George passed. To be honest, even his kisses had lost some of their intensity as we aged. My budding relationship with Mark is new and clearly exciting. I also tossed and turned knowing that I was going to be facing my friends this morning. I have considered a dozen ways to redirect their questions. I cross my fingers under the table before turning toward Betty with my answer. "Mark is no longer a murder suspect. He was not even in the country when John was killed. If I have my way, you will not see him kissing me in our lobby again. He will be kissing me in the privacy of my apartment where we will do as we please."

Betty's mouth hangs open; Hattie starts hooting as she slaps the table. "Good for you! May you get a little loving, and may it be fabulous. Of course, I will want details, but only if you want to share." By now the rest of the women around the table are laughing and clapping their hands. Betty still frowns as she closes her mouth.

"Now that we have gotten that out of the way, let's return to our investigation. What do we know and what do we still question?"

Myrtle is the first to kick things off, "As you know, you and I need to go back with our photo array. I think it may take three or four visits before we have found most of those residents on a good day. I don't have a high hope that any of them will recognize the man who may have visited John before his death."

I added, "On our next visit I want to test my theory about the keypad. I already know the numbers, and just need to check that nothing has changed when we are next punched in to the memory ward."

Hattie chimes in with, "The nursing staff at the Care Center really hasn't said anything new to help us."

"John had made so many withdrawals to give the money to that Xavier Onward Christian Ministry. Have we actually checked out the church? I thought we had discussed it, but I don't know what we had learned."

We all turn toward Betty. She is quickly paging back through her notes. "You are correct. We discussed them but we've not taken any action. This might be the time to do that."

"I'll start on that right away," Florence says.

"Clem told me that his son, Dean, shared details about his argument with his partner, Stan Mason. The forensic accountants are still looking at John and Elsie's bank records. They agree with Florence that someone other than John or Elsie made big withdrawals. They just haven't been able to determine who that might be. Stan is convinced that Mr. Johnson is the guilty party. Dean does not agree." Ethel frowns as she studies her hands. "I'm afraid that Dean won't be able to prevent Stan from bringing in Mr. Johnson for more questioning."

"It sounds like we have an action plan. Let's plan to meet again in two days. Surely by then we will know something important." I can only hope that those words come true.

Armed with the photo array of our suspects, Myrtle and I make the short drive to the Care Center. I don't know whether I am happy or sad that the access numbers have not changed. Once inside the memory ward, Penny greets us with her happy smile, giggle, and a quick clap of her hands. "Myrtle dear, you brought Mabel! It is so good to see both of you. What do you have there with you?"

"We brought you some pictures to look at. We are hoping you can tell us who you saw the day John was killed." Myrtle hands Penny the stack of pictures we have assembled. "Let me know if you recognize any of these men." I have my fingers crossed that today is a good day for Penny.

Holding up the picture of Brett, she says, "This is John's son. He came at least once a month I think, but never stayed long. I do remember that he was here the day that John died. I'm not sure just what time that was. I have problems with keeping days and time straight." I give her shoulder a quick squeeze. She continues, "And this one is John's son-in-law. I can't remember his name. He didn't come very often, and usually came with John's daughter. I think her name was Jane. They never came when Elsie was here. The only time I saw him with John's son, was the day John died." She skims through the other photos before holding up the one of Mark. "I've seen him here, but not in a very long time. Any man that looks this good is welcome to come back to visit me!" Penny adds her trademark giggle as she says this.

Wow! I had never considered that Brett and Don could have worked together to murder John. With luck we can get confirmation from at least one other resident that saw them together that day. That, however, proves to be something that might need to wait. Today was just not a good one for the other residents. Myrtle was correct about needing more than one visit with our photo array.

Chapter Thirty-Seven

There are times that I know I overthink making a simple decision. I need to pick a path, and right or wrong proceed rather than tossing and turning half the night second guessing myself. Inviting Mark to join me on an early morning walk should not be a life altering decision. He said he was an early morning person, so hopefully I won't wake him when I call. If he cannot join me today, maybe he can do so tomorrow. I have questions about our investigation that I think he may be able to answer. I need to know how he convinced Brett not to challenge the will. That was a detail that I had just filed away without giving it a second thought. Now that he is no longer a suspect, I look forward to sharing with him details about our investigation. Being honest with myself, I tossed and turned because I was raised to believe that proper women never call a man to ask him for a date. We always seem to have so much to talk about, and I want to know if he would be a good companion on my morning walks. Sheesh, now I'm making him sound like a dog I'm considering adopting!

My hands are sweaty as I pick up my phone. I'm not sure if I honestly hope he doesn't answer. Am I prepared to talk to his voice mail? I don't need to worry about that. "Good morning, Mabel. What a delightful way to start my day!"

"Good morning, Mark. I hope I'm not calling too early."

"Oh, no. I'm up and even had my first cup of coffee. You sound a bit tense. Is anything wrong? Is Elsie okay?"

"No, no. She is doing alright. I'm still concerned about the police and John's murder, but that is not why I'm calling. I am about ready to go for my morning walk, and wondered if you would like to join me?" There, I said it. It really wasn't that hard to do. I don't have to rely on the rules my mother drilled into me about proper behavior for a young woman. I haven't been a young woman in decades.

I realize that I have been holding my breath while I wait for Mark's answer. I release it as he says, "It is a beautiful day, and I'd love to join you. Do you want to walk from your apartment, or would you rather go somewhere special?"

"I hadn't considered anything special. Is there somewhere you like to walk?"

"How about I pick you up in 15 minutes, and we head to the beach. We can go for a nice breakfast after that. Will that work?"

I hadn't considered all of this, but it does sound nice. "The beach would be lovely. I haven't done that in ages. I'll be ready."

One of the delights about living in the Puget Sound area, is the selection of beaches within just a few miles of the St. James Apartments. Some of them offer rocks and tide pools brimming with marine life. Others have miles of sand that extends out when the tide is low. I'm really not sure why I don't go to the beach for walks more often. I honestly can't remember when I did this last. Walking hand and hand with Mark is just about perfect. I find it hard to remember just what I wanted to ask him. Focus, Mabel.

"Mark, I remember hearing John's son and son-in-law say they intended to challenge the will. How were you able to talk them out of it?"

"I started by pointing out how much it cost to have John in that nursing home before Medicaid kicked in. I had those details available because I had helped Elsie find that care center and apply for the Medicaid. The fact that John qualified quickly highlighted their financial situation."

"From the way Brett sounds in his interactions with Elsie, I thought he has been accusing her of hiding money.

Florence had totaled up the thousands of dollars that John had given to that ministry. Surely if Brett had known about that, he would understand why there was no money for her to hide."

"John's devotion to that group did put him in serious legal jeopardy as well as the potential for financial ruin. I could never understand what he was getting out of that relationship."

"Our group has decided we need to know more about them. I'm not sure we know where to start."

"Let me do a little checking on them. I really should have done more research on them. I assumed they were an online group located outside of Washington state, but I never really verified that even when John was working with them. I will let you know what I find out. Now let's go have a nice breakfast." John startles me when he raises our linked hands so he can kiss my knuckles. Wow! This man can be so romantic. Can I handle this?

Chapter Thirty-Eight

Ethel and Florence, followed closely by Hattie, all strut into my apartment looking like cats who have swallowed canaries. This might be an interesting way to start off this meeting of the investigative team. I know that Myrtle does not share that look. We have not had any success with our photos at the Care Center. Penny has been the only one who could identify any of the men in our photo array. We haven't given up hope, but it hasn't happened so far.

Betty looks up from her whiteboard and smiles as she says, "Oh goody, it looks like you three have something important to add to our investigation. I've got my pens arranged. Who's ready to start?"

Surprisingly Ethel and Hattie defer to Florence. "This was truly a team effort. We decided to take a close look at Brett and by extension his brother-in-law, Don, because Brett is just so nasty. We decided to stake out Brett's work and home, so that we could follow him. I am glad that my car is rather nondescript. It worked well for our stake out and following him. It didn't take many days before we could establish a pattern. Most afternoons he left work early, picked up Don, and drove up to the Muckleshoot Casino. We then took turns watching them inside the casino."

Hattie couldn't wait any longer, "I talked to the bar staff. Not only are the men there regularly, but they are heavy drinkers and even more heavy gamblers."

Ethel adds, "And they aren't very good gamblers. They lost thousands of dollars each night that we watched them. On another day we followed them to Emerald Downs. We didn't follow them in there but assume they are also betting on the horses. After the races, they continued on to the Casino."

"This may have been why," Florence adds, "Brett was always asking for money from his father."

"The fact that Don was there adds fuel to what Mark told me when he called this morning." I hope that my friends assume the smile that I can't hide whenever I say Mark's name, is due to the information he provided. "For the last four years, Brett, his sister, Jane, and her husband Don are the top three officers in the Xavier Onward Christian Ministry. The organization is chartered as a nonprofit, but each of these officers are paid a very healthy salary. Mark said he intended to do more digging in the hopes that he can find out how the Ministry money is spent. He added that he should have spent time investigating them when John's work for them became an issue at the firm."

Betty looks up from her notebook. She has been organizing our reports before adding them to our whiteboards. "Has anyone ever asked Elsie what these children do for a living?"

I realize I should've asked Elsie more questions when I was asking her about her marriage to John. "Elsie did tell me that Jane did not work. She said Don was very much like John in that he insisted that Jane stay home and keep house."

"And people wonder why I never married," Betty mumbles. "I never wanted a man who would tell me what I could or couldn't do."

Myrtle smiles as she says, "My dear friend, Elmer, told me that Brett and Don own that used car lot not far from his fruit stand. He also said they do not have a very good reputation with other business owners in the area."

"His fruit stand is in North Renton by the airport, isn't it?"

"That's right."

"Florence, have you actually met Brett and Don, other than seeing them at the funeral?"

"That was the only place. I was not involved when Brett was here making that fuss at Elsie. Why do you ask?"

"I'm thinking that we need to have you go car shopping. None of the rest of us can go with you nor can Diana because we have all met him in person. Do you think Rosa would be willing to go with you as an escort for safety?"

Florence looks almost shocked. She looks around at all of us, "Are you saying that you think Brett and Don are involved in John's murder?"

"That's exactly what I'm saying, and it is the reason I don't want you there by yourself. I'm not sure what all you can glean from them, but I think we need all of the information that we can get. That's why I want you to take Rosa with you." Although Rosa Hatfield is not part of our investigative group, she is a good fifteen years younger than Florence. I also know that while I go for morning walks, Rosa goes to a local gym where she works out. She teaches self-defense classes there. That combination should keep Florence as safe as we can make her.

"I'll need to share with her what we have been doing. If there's an issue, she will need to be as prepared as possible."

"If you can add anything to our investigation, it may be just what we need to convince the police that we have discovered the real murderers." Just saying that gives me cold shivers up and down my spine.

Chapter Thirty-Nine

Myrtle and I chat as we make the drive to the Care Center. I can program my GPS by simply telling it where I wish to go. I feel that at this point I should be able to do the same with my car, because it should know the route to the Care Center by heart. We have made this trip so many times in the last few weeks. I realize I am trying to avoid thinking about Florence and Rosa on their spying trip to that used car lot. I can only hope that my bright idea has not put my friends in danger. "Myrtle, do you think we will have better luck today having one of Penny's neighbors recognize anyone from our photos?"

"Today may be a good day for that. Since our investigation has eliminated the possibility of a crazy nurse, we should be safe. I can only hope that Florence and Rosa will also be safe. You do think that sending them there was a good plan, don't you?"

"There really shouldn't be any reason for them to be in danger. Florence has Hattie on speed dial. Hattie knows to have her phone charged and on. She will quickly call 911. If Florence has a problem, she only needs to press one button for help. We all agreed that we must have just a little bit more information before Diana can take what we know to Stan Mason. That information has to be about Brett and Don because they are the only ones who could have killed John."

As frequently occurred in the past, there is no one at the desk with the sign-in book. Again, I am struck by how easy it would be for someone to enter the memory ward without any record of them doing so. "Myrtle, let's run a test. We will go ahead and sign in, and then enter the memory ward without an escort."

"Works for me."

Myrtle keeps watch as I quickly enter the four numbers in the order that I have observed in the past. The keypad light changes from red to green and we hear the door unlatch. As always, Penny is parked in her chair ready to greet us. A quick look down the hall confirms that there is not a nurse in sight to observe our entry. I turn to give Penny a big smile. "Penny, you are looking bright and cheery. Is that a new dress?"

"I'm glad you like it. It is just a dress that has been hanging in the back of my closet. I don't know why I haven't been wearing it." The dress in question has big yellow and green flowers all over it. It is bright, but I can't say it is attractive. I can see, however, that Penny is happy that I noticed.

Myrtle turns Penny's chair, and begins to push her down the hall toward her room. "So has anything new happened since the last time we came to visit?"

"Myrtle, you should know by now that in a nursing home nothing really changes. One of my neighbors did say that he hoped you would come back for another visit. I told him that you were my friend not his. Are you still asking questions about John?" By now Penny and Myrtle have reached Penny's room. We had agreed beforehand that I would continue on with our photo array in hopes of speaking with Penny's neighbors.

The door to the next room is open. The plaque beside the door gives the room number and below that the name Mike Nesbitt. I see the man I assume is Mike Nesbitt watching television. *Should I call him 'Mike' as if he is an old friend or should I use 'Mr. Nesbitt'?* I hope I have made the correct decision. "Hi Mike, how are you doing today?"

Mike turns to look at me with a confused expression on his face. He almost growls as he says, "You are not one of those damn nurses. Why are you asking me how I'm doing today?"

Oh dear, this is not off to a very good start. This might be a good time to just tell the truth. "You are correct; I am not one of the nurses. I am a friend of Penny's from next door, and I hoped to show you some pictures of men who might have been to see John just before he died. May I show them to you?"

"Well, I can't see them from there, so get your ass over here and pull up a chair."

I am hopeful that being rude is a good sign with this man rather than a phase in his dementia. I take the chair that is already sitting next to him. I slowly hand him our photos one at a time. He studies each of them carefully before setting two of them aside. The rest he hands back to me. "Before I ended up here, I had been a police detective. I have done the same exercise with other people, but never has anyone done this with me. Exactly what do you want to know about these two bozos?"

His response startles me. "You recognize them?"

"Of course, they were always yelling at John when they were here. The last time they were here the yelling stopped quickly. I walked over to my doorway to see them skedaddling through the locked door. My police training told me they were up to no good. My memory issues stepped in, and I couldn't even tell one of those damn nurses. I can't even tell you how long ago I saw that. I hate it, but I can't control it. Do you think it was connected to John's death?"

I quickly realize I should have recorded this discussion. As I say, "Yes, I do. And I intend to tell the police about it." The words are no more out of my mouth, then Mr. Nesbitt's expression changes to an angry one.

"What are you doing in my room? I don't know you. Get out of here!" Out in the hallway I pull up my phone to make a note of the date, the time, and what Mr. Nesbitt told me. He may not be the best eyewitness, but this might be enough for Diana to take to Stan Mason. She needs to convince them to take a closer look at Brett and Don.

Chapter Forty

Myrtle and I agree that this information calls for an emergency meeting of the investigative team. As I drive us back to the St. James, she sends out text messages to everyone adding Diana and Rosa to the group. She set the meeting for my apartment in an hour. Within minutes she gets replies from everyone except Florence and Rosa. I keep asking if she has heard from them, and she keeps shaking her head until we pull in to the parking lot at the St. James. Her answer is still no, as the team takes their places around my table. Diana is the first to ask, "Where is Florence?"

I feel both scared and guilty as I tell her, "She and Rosa went to Brett's used car lot supposedly looking for a car, but were really looking for clues."

"Have you heard from them since they left?"

It is Hattie's turn, "Rosa sent me a text just after they arrived. She told me that both Brett and Don were at the car lot. Their plan was that Rosa would be outside looking at cars once they saw both Don and Brett come out of the office building. Florence was to ask about using the restroom as a reason to be inside. I've heard nothing from them since then."

Ethel looks at first Myrtle and then at me before asking, "Is this why you called an emergency meeting?"

"We didn't know about this. We had a man at the Care Center who identified Brett and Don. He said he was a former police detective and that he had seen the two men as he said, 'skedaddle' after they had been shouting at John. I took notes about what he said, but really wished I had recorded him. Diana, we wanted something more concrete that you could take to Stan Mason in the hopes he would look at Brett and Don rather than Elsie and Mr. Johnson."

Just then Hattie's phone chirps with an incoming text. She glances at the screen before looking at all of us. "It's from Rosa. There's nothing but an H. That was our code for help."

I instantly pick up my keys before saying to the group, "Quickly grab your purses and pepper spray if you have it. If we all go to that car lot, there should be safety in numbers."

I hear one of our members say, "It'll only take me a minute to pee when I pick up my purse." The elevator door closes before I can lock my door. I'll need to wait for it to come back up.

Diana is still in the hallway. I hear her on the phone. "Stan, I think we may need your help. Two of the women from the St. James may be in trouble. We have reason to believe that Brett and Don might have been the ones who murdered John. I am not making this up to protect my client!" I can only pray that we get to that car lot in time. She turns to me, "Can you forward me your notes? From the response he just gave me, I know it will take more than one phone call to get him to act. I'll stay here to keep pushing Stan. Let me know if I need to call the Renton police." She has that warrior look again as she joins me in the elevator going down.

The eight miles from the St. James to North Renton goes by in a blur. I conclude that I may have been driving a little too fast when I make the sharp turn into the used car lot. All of my friends have given a squeal that almost matches the sound from my tires. They still manage to climb out quickly once I come to a full stop. Betty, Ethel, and Hattie head in different directions in the lot while Myrtle and I march toward the office. If Florence and Rosa are being held as captives, it most certainly would be in the office. The second we open the door, we hear a commotion coming from one of the rooms in the back. We rush into the room, but stop in our tracks just inside the doorway. Brett is lying face down on the floor with Rosa sitting on his back. She has a wooden plaque held over her head with both hands. Brett appears to be out cold, so I assume she must have given him a whack. Don is backed into a corner with his hands up as Florence stands three feet away with her pepper spray aimed at his face. I don't know whether to laugh or cheer. We little old ladies aren't as defenseless as most people assume. I hear sirens in the street outside. I know that Rosa and Florence will need to be giving statements for the next hour or so. My phone chimes with a text from Diana, 'Stan and Dean are on their way.' The five of us will stay with Florence and Rosa until we know for sure that our work here is done. I'll give Diana a call with an update once we know what Stan Mason intends to do.

Epilogue

Stepping in to the banquet room makes me think I have stepped into a time machine. Three Dog Night with 'Joy to the World' is blasting from the sound system. If cigarette smoke had been rolling out the door, I would swear I was back in the VFW where the local dances were held when I was a teenager. I can hear Hattie adding "Jeremiah was a bullfrog" to every verse even though that is not the lyrics. I will bet that she is the one who selected the music. All of the women who live in the building appear to be here and actively singing or cheering. The noise is almost deafening.

Mr. Johnson is on one side of the room surrounded by a number of our residents. Elsie is on the other side of the room turned away from Mr. Johnson. The members of our investigative team are still giving Elsie hugs and each other high fives. Myrtle has pulled Florence out into the middle of the room to dance. I look over at Mr. Johnson to confirm that he has his arm draped across the shoulders of the new young thing who had moved into an apartment on the fourth floor. I haven't met her personally, but have only heard her mentioned by others who live on her floor. Okay, I can't really say she is a 'new young thing.' A woman in her early 70s is truly no longer young. She has only lived in the building for a few weeks. She is looking up at Mr. Johnson in adoration. Does this mean that Elsie and Mr. Johnson are no longer an item? I have not been expecting this.

As I approach Elsie's group, I hear her say to Hattie, "You're absolutely right. I don't regret the time I spent with Zeb in the least. To be honest, despite two marriages, I didn't know that sex could be fun. If I'm going to have a relationship at this age, I think I want something more like what Ethel has with Clem. It seems to have a base of respect and friendship. I'm afraid Zeb will always be looking for his next adventure." I add an extra squeeze to the hug I give Elsie. She has been through so much and despite what she says now, I'm afraid she's going to miss Zeb's company more than she realizes.

Rosa shakes her finger at me. "The next time you decide to organize an investigative team, I expect to be one of the first members. You all need to join my self-defense class, because without that training I could not have taken Brett down so easily."

"I need to call a meeting for the team at my apartment where it is not quite so noisy for you to give us all of those details. I still can't believe you knocked him out cold." I think I will need to make a point of going back to the Care Center to give both Penny and Mike Nesbitt an update on our investigation. Without their input, we might never have figured out the clues.

The door to the party room opens at the same time there is a change in the music to Freddie Mercury and 'We Are the Champions.' The noise level goes up as all of the women start to sing along. I can't hear what Diana says to Dean nor Ethel to Clem. Both men seem to be pleased to be here. I can only hope that Stan Mason does not put in an appearance.

I don't hear the door open again, but I suddenly feel Mark's hands on my shoulders. I feel a thrill as he whispers in my ear, "I had no idea that you ladies were such wild party animals. You never cease to amaze me."

I don't care who's watching. I wrap my arms around his waist as he pulls me in for a close hug. He whispers in my ear something about a trip away for a few nights to celebrate. I like that idea. This feels like a special moment. That moment is broken when Myrtle pulls on my arm to join our friends as we sing and dance to Helen Reddy and 'I am Woman.' We may not be good singers, but we do know how to roar. Maybe this should be our theme song. As the song ends, Diana gives a very shrill and unladylike whistle.

The noise dies down quickly, and even Hattie goes over to turned down the music. Diana has taken that warrior stance even though she is in jeans and a T-shirt. She uses what I identify as her courtroom voice as she says, "Dean Swanson just shared that it is official. Neither Elsie nor Mr. Johnson are implicated in John Hansen's death. His son, Brett Hansen, and son-in-law, Don Spencer, have been arrested for his murder. You ladies should be proud of yourselves. I should scold you for putting any of your group in harm's way, but I think Rosa is correct, we all need to take her self-defense class!" We applaud as Hattie turns up the music, and the party continues.

An hour later the only sounds are those of dishes being washed in the kitchen by our team members as we talk quietly among ourselves. Rosa has promised to come for tea tomorrow and give us the details about what took place in the used-car office. Florence says she's not sure she wants to ever relive that experience, but she may change her mind by tomorrow. Dean and Clem have taken Ethel out for dinner to celebrate. Mark gave me a kiss on my cheek when he left about ten minutes ago. He did say he would call me later. I hope he doesn't wait too long, because I have a feeling, I'm going to fall asleep quickly tonight. Our group looks tired, but we all share big smiles as we wait for the elevator. We did what we set out to do. As soon as the elevator doors open, Gloria Wilson steps out with a panicky look on her face. She says "I just got a call from my daughter. She told me my granddaughter appears to be missing, and the police don't seem to take it seriously. Can you help?" *Oh dear. We did save Mr. Johnson. Will this be another case for the St. James Lady Detectives?*

About Alyne Bailey

Alyne Bailey often told her community college business students that she intended to write something other than textbooks. After her retirement and move from Washington state to Texas, she has been able to do just that. "It has been so much fun using a life time of the interesting people I have met and their life stories as inspiration for my romance novels. It is like getting to know those people all over again." Red Straw Hat on a Beach is her fourth book in her Red Hats in Love series.

Social Media

Facebook: https://www.facebook.com/alynebailey.author/
Twitter: https://twitter.com/AlyneBailey @alynebailey
Goodreads:
https://www.goodreads.com/author/show/19977036.Alyne_Bailey
Website: https://alynebailey.com/

Acknowledgements

Writing a book, is hard work. As always, there are so many times I question why I'm putting myself through the efforts. Then I step back and think about the reviews and comments from my faithful readers. The encouragement you give me, is just what I need to keep pushing to put words onto the page. Thank you. Your reviews mean a great deal to me.
When I wrote Red Hard Hat in Construction, I looked back to my younger self when I lived in two different apartment buildings filled with ladies in their 80's. The women were

both interesting and fun. As I created the St James Apartment Building and the women who lived there, I pictured my great aunts and my mother's older friends. They inspired me to believe I was not too old to do something new. I could even write romance novels! When I decided to give these ladies their own book, I came to a shocking discovery. If these women were my great aunts, their stories would have taken place in World War 1. They would now be at least 125 years old! A 75-year-old woman living in this building would be my age! Clearly, my timelines needed to be adjusted to tell their stories. My aunt told me that she met her first husband when the USO bus got stuck in the mud and needed to be pulled out by a team of horses just after WW1 ended. The story was too good not to share. The bus could be stuck during the Korean War. I could ignore the horses. As I continue to tell their stories, I realize that women have faced many of the same issues over the last 150 years. The world around us may appear to change, but older women still struggle to find our place in that world.

I want to thank Nancy Howard for her ongoing patience and support as she reads and then re-reads my rough drafts. I wonder if she notices that there are fewer times that she needs to point out missing commas with each book?

I want to thank Gerry Eugene, poet and storyteller extraordinaire (*Seeing Things)*, for challenging me to write a mystery rather than a romance. He stated that he might actually read my mystery where he only ever plans to give away my romance books. I wasn't sure I could do it, but now I see at least one more cozy mystery in my future. There will be more romance efforts down the road, but writing cozy mysteries means I get to spend more time with the St James Apartment ladies that I love. The 2nd cozy mystery - *Finding Sarah Winters* is now a work in progress.

Jill Hawkins was indispensable in providing technical knowledge of senior care centers and memory care. Thank you, Jill.

Thank you to Kathi and Melissa of Solstice Publishing for all of your hard work. I am delighted to be part of your team.

Thank you also to the real Mabel Schmidel. I see you and hear you in my head as I design new adventures and problems for you to solve. I hope you would have approved.

Made in the USA
Monee, IL
06 July 2023